# BIKER BAIT

THE LOST SOULS MC - BOOK ONE

ELLIE R HUNTER

Ellie R Hunter

Biker Bait



Self-publishing

ellierhunter@hotmail.co.uk



Editing – Rebel & Edit Design

Cover Designer – Tracie Douglas

Formatting – Rachael Tonks

# BIKER BAIT

THE LOST SOULS MC- BOOK ONE

ELLIE R. HUNTER

# PROLOGUE

The gavel hits the table with force, ending our club meeting. Just as everyone is getting up to go their separate ways, our President, Michael "Tornado" Blake, orders us to sit again.

"One last bit of business, boys," he announces, rising from his chair at the head of the table.

"As you all know, Alannah is coming home next week. I've decided she won't be staying here. I've set up a place for her in town, and she'll lead a civilian life, away from the club."

As soon as he's finished, Oak and Sparky are out of their seats, arguing over each other to get a word in. In the end, Oak wins, and Sparky shuts up.

"You can't fuckin' do that to her. This is all she knows," he spits, looking our President square in the eye.

"I can and I will. It's not all she knows anymore. She's been away on and off for four years at college. She'll survive."

"Why are you doing this? She hated every day at college and you know it," Oak argues.

"It doesn't matter. I've made my decision, and it's fuckin' final."

"What about a vote?" Sparky speaks up.

"It's not club business, it's my family business. I'm letting you all know because she's going to go batshit crazy, and I don't need you fucks kicking off as well. I'm allowing her the ride home instead of flying, and I don't want you bunch of shits telling her. I'll tell her myself."

"This is bullshit," Sparky swears, slumping back into his chair.

Oak remains standing, bristling with anger. I know how close he is to Alannah, and this isn't going to help club morale. In my brother's eyes, she can do no wrong.

"I second that. You're putting her out for nothing and straight into the arms of the Raging Riders. She won't be safe!" Oak roars.

"This is final, and I won't be fuckin' questioned about it. But you can rest assure, she will be safe. She'll have a prospect posted near her at all times. Now, Sparky, you still need to do the run before you pick her up," he says with such authority, it renders them both silent.

Sparky nods, while Oak continues to scowl.

"Do we have a problem, old friend?"

He continues to stare for so long, I start to believe there will be a problem. Eventually, he shakes his head and starts for the door. With his hand on the door handle, he turns and speaks for the final time.

"I'll be joining Sparky on the run, bringing our girl home where she belongs, even if it is for a few days."

A few of the others murmur their agreement and begin filing out of the room. I remain seated as Michael sits back down.

"Anything to add, VP?"

What could I say? Deep down, I was just as angry as the others at our President's decision, but on the outside, I keep my cool and light up a cigarette.

"Absolutely nothing," I say, blowing out the smoke.

"Good." I hate the look on his face. It screams that he's hiding something. "I want you on the run too. Make sure the ride back is clear."

"You got it." I smile falsely, standing.

I leave the room, angrier than I was before. I hate the fact that I'm trusted with this girl's life on the road, just as long as it's not on the back of my bike.

9 Months Ago

Alannah

My summer break was coming to an end, and I was about to get a going away present I would never forget. A night with Castiel "Cas" Jackson, recently promoted to Vice President of the Lost Souls MC, and all-around sex on legs. We'd spent the entire summer together when he wasn't on club business, each day becoming closer and closer. In the beginning, I assumed he was just being nice to a brother's niece like all the rest, becoming a brother to me, until I saw the changes. Sly touches here and there. The way I would catch him watching me with his lopsided grin when he thought I wasn't looking. It soon became clear—or I thought it did—that he felt the same as I did about him.

The day before I was due to leave for my last year of college, we shared—again, I thought we shared—an urgent need to be together. Every member of the Lost Souls had been warned with violence and being put to ground if they came near me with carnal thoughts in mind. I believed at the time I could talk to my uncle and show him I wasn't being used like the club sluts. That what Cas and I shared was real.

I barely noticed the concerned glances from the men I called family as I walked through the clubhouse. John "Oak" Johnson stood from his place at the bar, but was pulled back down by his drinking partner.

Thinking nothing of it, I carried on, walking toward Cas's room. I was nervous and eager at the same time. I felt dangerous. I spent longer than usual showering and blow drying my long, blonde hair. It fell in long, soft curls, and unlike the whores who hung around the club, I kept my make-up minimal with just enough black eyeliner to set my blue eyes off, the way I knew Cas liked it. The cutoff denim shorts I had chosen gave the illusion of my legs being longer than they were for my five-foot four-inch frame, and the tight-fitting tee showed my curves in all the right places. My hand on the doorknob to his room surprised me by shaking, and before my nerves got the better of me, I slowly opened his door.

What I saw, I knew would haunt me for a very long time. Cas was definitely in his room, but so was Danni, one of the club whores. Sitting on his lap, her short skirt pulled up around her waist and her top pulled down. From what I could tell, she was in the middle of climaxing. I expected for him to at least look guilty at being caught, but he didn't. Instead, he put his hands on her hips and pumped into her, never taking his eyes away from mine as he came. My heart not only broke, it smashed into so many pieces, no man would ever be able to put it back together again. I don't know what kept me rooted to the spot in his doorway. Pain, I guess? I couldn't move until the whore turned and saw me. She didn't know what had gone on between us all summer, but the satisfying smile of banging the Vice President made me want to scratch her eyes out.

Cas remained on his bed, reaching for his smokes.

"Do you mind? We don't want an audience," Danni snapped. "Isn't it past your bedtime? Leave, or do you need me to show you out?" she laughed as she sat beside Cas, her hand draped over his bare chest.

Her threat brought me out of my trance. What I had just witnessed would take hours, days, even weeks to figure out. It was obvious I held no power when it came to Cas, but if she thought she could talk to me, Alannah Blake, like she just did and get away with it, she was more stupid than I gave the club whores credit for.

"You know what? I'm not sure. Why don't we go ask my uncle, the President of the brother you just fucked?" Her smile vanished, and she visibly paled.

I was begging myself to not let them see how hurt I was. I

jerked my chin up higher and gathered every ounce of dignity I had left.

"In fact, why don't we go and tell my uncle, the *President*, how a club whore just threatened me. I don't think he'll be too pleased."

"I–I'm sorry, I didn't know who you were. I'm so sorry," she rambled on, scrambling off the bed and adjusting her clothes. As she passed me on her way out, she apologised again, then asked me not to say anything. These girls made me sick, hanging around men who would never make them their old ladies because they had slept with most of the club. With that thought, I realised that that was how Cas saw me. Humiliated, I ran from his room, failing to compose myself before making it to the bar area in the club. Everyone's eyes were on me as I left.

This time, Oak stood and grabbed my wrist as I passed. He spoke gently, but loud enough for anyone in the room to hear. It was a promise to me, and a threat to everyone else.

"This is the only time I see you cry, Barbie. Next time, someone goes to ground, and I don't care if he is a brother."

Not trusting myself to speak, I nodded and left when he released my arm. I loved Oak like a father. He always had a soft spot for me, and when my father died, he, along with my uncle, stepped up and made sure I didn't go without anything.

My uncle owned the house on the edge of the compound where we lived. I couldn't run fast enough across the lot and to my room. My uncle greeted me at the door, no doubt already knowing what had happened, like everyone else.

"He's not for you," was all I heard from my uncle as I

pounded up the stairs, letting the pain take me as it all sunk in.

The next morning, everyone came out to say their goodbyes before I left for college on the back of Sparky's bike. I acted like nothing had happened, and so did they. As I got on the bike and clasped my fingers together around Sparky's waist, I caught Cas standing in the shadows of the garage, watching, his face showing no emotion. Needless to say, he didn't come out to say goodbye, and I certainly made no effort to do so either.

# 1

## Alannah

Thank God, my last year of college is finished. I can relax now, knowing I'm going home. I couldn't wait to hit the road, and I'd been counting down the days until I got to go home since the beginning of the year. My home has made me the young woman I am today. Looking around at everyone packing their cars for summer break, I wonder how they cope with what they consider their "normal" and "conventional" lives. Me, I'm the niece of Michael "Tornado" Blake, President of the Lost Souls Motorcycle Club, and daughter of Mark "Boss" Blake, previous President and founder of the Lost Souls before he died. My mother was the love of my father's life, but died while giving birth to me. Apart from attending college—at my uncle's insistence—there's nothing outsiders would consider normal or conventional about my life, and that's okay. I would rather choke on stale ale than live like them.

No longer able to wait in my dorm room as instructed, I jump on the curb from one foot to the other in anticipation of my ride home. It's not until I hear the loud rumble of the only Harley I want to ride upon that my heart skips that much faster. I immediately squash the building fire in my lower tummy. How can I still feel a need for someone so cruel? Composing myself rapidly, I lean against the railing, hiding the hurt in my eyes he caused me behind my sunglasses. This summer, I'm not going to fall for the Vice President. Not again.

Uncle Mike wanted me to fly home and pick me up himself from the airport, but I had other ideas. I wanted to ride home, to blow away the academic year on the road, but I wasn't prepared for what I saw turning the corner. It's not only Sparky who's come, but nine of the other brothers too. Blasting their horns, I choke up. My family has come to take me home. Glancing around, people are sneaking looks at the bikes and the men riding them. I giggle to myself. They always look scared, like they're going to be mugged, roughed up, or worse. To me, they're just my brothers and uncles. Sure, the world they live in isn't where you'd find a suit working nine to five each day. Far from it. They have their dealings in weapons, drugs, and protection, but when it comes to one of the family, you couldn't find more loyal people. They would die for one another, and fight to the death for the club. To me, the code they live by and the way they are is the hottest thing I see on a day-to-day basis.

One by one, they cut their engines and depart their bikes,

whooping and cheering, congratulating me on finishing college. I pull away from the railing when I see Pope advancing toward me. He's one of the quieter brothers, and my Uncle Michael's Sergeant-at-Arms. At over six and a half feet in height, and over two hundred and fifty pounds, nobody has ever taken his quietness for weakness. His long black beard is tied with a band today, and so is his long hair. He would now greet me with respect for my uncle, and wouldn't say another word to me until I spoke to him, or he needed to ask me something, which was never. I used to take offence until I realised he was the same with everyone. He only says what he needs to say, and that's it. Sparky, my uncle's Road Chief, and the closest thing I have to a real brother, rushes over and lifts me into his arms, swinging me around. The chains hanging from his leathers clink against each link, and his cut smells of home. Unlike the majority of the brothers, Sparky keeps his hair shaved short. I think he likes for everyone to see his tattoos snaking around his neck and up onto his head. See, most girls would be put off with markings like that, but for me, tattoos are a big turn on.

"Hey, Barbs. We missed you," he says as he releases me, placing me back on my feet.

"If you didn't bring me back here, you wouldn't have had to miss me," I retort, following him back to his bike.

"I don't make the rules, kid." He pulls out a spare helmet from his side bag. "Now, if you want to make it home before dark, get on."

I desperately want to be home. I'm embraced and greeted by each of the guys before I realise it's Cas who is next. I know he doesn't want to hug me, or even congratulate me, or even welcome me home. His show is exactly that—a show. Quickly, I turn away from his six foot, tanned, tied up dark brown hair, make-you-melt body. I'm not going near him, because I can't afford the flood of hate and need that follow. Sparky had told me he was picking me up on the way back from a run, so it wasn't like Cas had specifically come to get me.

I clasp my helmet in place and climb on behind Sparky, wrapping my arms tight around his waist. I know everyone saw the disrespect I'd shown the Vice President, but I don't care. I'll deal with the repercussions of it after I get home.

Sparky holds my hand at his front for a few seconds longer than usual, gives it a squeeze, and proceeds to start his bike.

"Ready to get the hell out of here, Barbie?" he shouts over the roar of the bikes.

"Hell yeah," I cheer through my laughter.

Unless you've been on a Harley, you can't imagine how it feels. I squeeze my legs around Sparky with excitement. I love to ride, to feel free. It just feels amazing.

Catching Cas's eye as he passes us makes me nervous. His face is a carefully composed mask. I suppose I'll find out when we get back what he thinks of my shunning him. I push all thoughts of him out of my mind as everyone pulls out in order of their rank within the club.

I'm giddy with excitement. I'm going home for good.

**Cas**

Who the fuck does she think she is, blatantly disrespecting

me in front of my club? It doesn't matter if I deserve it or not. She knows the rules, and she certainly knows what happens when a brother is disrespected.

I scold myself. I'm not jealous that she's on the back of Sparky's bike and not mine. I tell myself I'm angry she's on a bike at all, especially after her earlier insult to me—the VP.

For days, all I've heard is Alannah's name. Everyone's excitement at her homecoming, the old ladies planning the biggest party the club has seen in months, and the glares from my brothers, warning me not to get close again.

In the beginning, I was angry with myself for hurting her. The look on her face when she saw me with whatever her name was, plagued me for months. I took every hit my brothers threw at me that night so I could be with her before my hand was forced in other ways. Then I got angry. There were no consequences for Little Miss Tight-Ass. She knew a Lost Souls member wasn't allowed near her, and she still enticed me with her fresh pussy and tight body. She nearly cost me my fucking position in the club and my family. I'm not connected to my brothers by blood, but they are my family, and I would die for each and every one of them.

Halfway home, we stop to refill the tanks and to stretch our legs before the last half of our journey. Alannah disappears into the store with Slade while I remain by my bike.

I pull my pack of cigarettes out of my pocket and light one up.

"You okay, brother?" Sparky, the brother I'm closest to in the club, questions, coming up beside me.

He lights a cigarette as he waits for my reply.

"I'm good. Just want to be home."

"I feel you. It's been a long few days," he agrees.

Indeed, it has been. The monthly run was meant to take minimal time and effort. Instead, it nearly ended in a free-for-all fight until Oak stepped in and talked us all down. The Raging Riders have been causing a lot trouble for us and our supporting MC's, and the friction is starting to come to a head.

The excitement oozing from him now is tangible. He wants to mention Alannah and how happy he is she's coming home, but he won't because of what I did. No one speaks to me about her anymore. The most conversation I take part in concerning her is as a third person. No more than I deserve, but still. The sooner we get back, the sooner I can fuck off.

She comes strutting out of the store, licking on an ice cream. The image of her flicking her tongue like that on my cock has me turning and covering my lower half behind my bike. Fucking bitch. I can't be getting hard every time she does something—something anyone else would do, but not be nearly as hot while doing it. I focus on the anger I have toward her for breaking the rules as much as I did and not getting punished for it.

She looks toward me as she passes, her eyebrows pulling together quickly before looking away. Her hips, with their natural sway, has me throbbing as she makes her way to Sparky's bike. Fuck this shit. I whistle, letting the guys know it's time to ride on.

Raising my hand, I signal to my brothers that we're home. Horns could be heard all over the small town of Willow's Peak. Cheers erupted as the gates opened at our arrival to our compound, welcoming home the princess who can do no fucking wrong. I start toward where our bikes are kept while Sparky carries on, taking Alannah straight into the middle of the party. I stay put as I watch them disappear into the crowd.

"Any problems on the ride back?"

I turn to see my President coming up behind me, looking more tired and worn-down than usual.

"Nah. Clear run all the way back," I tell him.

His eyes dart between me and the crowd where Alannah is. He doesn't have to say anything. I know my place, and I'm not prepared to lose it over forbidden fucking pussy.

"Come on, I need to get fucking wasted," I grunt, heading toward the clubhouse.

I barely make it to the bar before one of the club groupies is hanging off my arm, giggling in my ear.

I give her only half of my attention until I see she's a newbie, and she's hot. She would do for tonight at least. I pull her onto my lap and stroke her arm. Just as I'm beginning to relax, I hear the voice I wish would fuck off back to college.

"Good to see nothing changes around here."

I glare at her. Her presence and her sarcasm are not welcome.

"Hey, darlin', why don't you go and wait in my room for me," I tell the hang-around.

I give her my room number and key before shoving her off my lap. Once she's gone, I look at Alannah properly for the first time since she's been back. Her hair has grown longer, nearly reaching the middle of her back. I wonder what it would feel like to wrap my fist around it. Her already toned, tight midriff seems even tauter, brushing against her tight tee. It doesn't need my imagination to know how perky her tits are underneath.

"Stare much?" she quips.

"What do you want?"

"I came to apologise to the Vice President. Apparently, I was rude earlier."

Her apology might be believable if it weren't for the fact it was dripping with sarcasm, or her usual soft features weren't replaced with repulsion. She's only apologising because she's been made to, and I'm fine with that. I want to admit her sassy mouth is making me twitch. I want to admit I want her in my room, eagerly awaiting my cock. Rearranging my thoughts, and my bulge, I stand up and get in her face, as close as I'm allowed to, but it's a mistake. She smells so good.

I keep my poker face intact and snarl,

"Fuck your apology. Just stay out of my way."

I stare at her, daring her to make a comeback. She holds my gaze, but says nothing, so I walk away, leaving her frozen in place and feeling like shit.

### Alannah

He really is a jerk. I hate him, and I hate my uncle for making me apologise. He heard of my earlier shun toward Cas, and niece or not, I had to say I was sorry. It could've been worse, I suppose. I've seen people barred from hanging around the club for less shows of disrespect.

I don't know why I was surprised to see a whore hanging off him when I approached. Whores attract whores, and he's one of the biggest manwhores out there. I guess some things will never change. Well, it's obvious he still doesn't care about anyone but himself, and I didn't expect that to be any different. There were a few nights while at college, I fantasised about him turning up on his bike and begging for my forgiveness, but those eventually passed. The harsh reality would return, and I would end up crying myself to sleep.

Exhaling the breath I didn't realise I was holding, I turn in a circle, finding we have an audience. I won't let them see me crumble again, not over Cas Jackson.

Plastering on a smile, I raise my head and shout,

"Let's get this party started!"

Cheers and conversations resume, and I'm pulled toward the bar where the drinks are flowing, the music's cranked up, and my homecoming celebration is in full swing.

This is where I belong, with big, burly bikers, their forever forgiving old ladies, and to an extent, the club whores—not that I give them much of my time.

I'm sure my uncle has different ideas for me. His earlier "we'll talk tomorrow" didn't set me at ease. For the past year, he hasn't hidden his feelings about wanting a different way of life for me. There have been cryptic mumbles here and there when I've visited home on school breaks.

"Here's to you, darlin'. So fuckin' proud of you," Oak beams, grinning from ear to ear as he pushes a beer toward me.

"Thanks," I grin back, taking a healthy swig before he pulls me in for a hug, which from a big ass biker, hurts.

"Alannah, come here!" I peek over Oak's shoulder to see Aunt Kitty calling me over, where shots of Tequila are lined up on the bar in front of her. For a bunch of women in their late thirties to forties, they can still hold their liquor. Old ladies rarely party at the clubhouse, but tonight is different.

It was hard not to stay in a party mood with their wild enthusiasm bouncing around, but what Michael said earlier kept running through my head.

When the Tequila kicks in and my party mood completely evaporates, I slip out of the clubhouse and climb quietly up the old stairs to the club's roof, the one place I'm able to think in peace. I can still hear the music and laughter, but up here, I can pretend no one is around.

I knew it would be awkward on my first night back with Cas around. At college, it was easy to forget about him, but here, I was fooling myself that I could escape him. I promise myself I'll do my damnedest to stay away from him.

I have to.

I love the club.

I've grown up not knowing any different, but I'm not stupid. I know my place, and as a woman, even as the niece of the notorious Michael Blake, my place is way down in the ranks, even below the old lady status. It doesn't mean I'm not loved as much, or respected and treated well. I just know that if my uncle decides to send me somewhere for my benefit and the good of the club, I would have to go, and that would absolutely kill me. His constant digs about me having more than the club were screaming at me. Is he trying to prepare me for something?

Sighing, I look up at the stars, pondering what my fate will be.

"It's good to have you home, Barbie."

I nod at Sparky as he steps onto the roof. Making his way over, he lays down beside me.

"Might not be my home after tomorrow," I mumble, not bothering to look at him.

"This will always be your home. Don't go worrying about that," he assures me.

"Do you know what's going to happen to me?"

"You'll know when you need to know."

I knew he wouldn't tell me. That's how the club works, everyone working on a need-to-know basis.

The smell of his leather cut and the beer on his breath is comforting. I remember my first year at college, feeling weird because I missed the smell of leather and oil, and any other aroma that reminded me of home. College didn't smell even remotely the same.

"Thanks for coming to visit me while I was away," I tell him sincerely. I valued each and every time he came to see me. He gave me a little piece of home in a place that resembled nothing of it.

"It was nothing. Couldn't leave you too long on your own. You might have come back in a Prius or something." He shuddered at the idea.

I laughed at the thought. No one could make me laugh like Sparky.

"As if, jackass. Are you sure you can't tell me what's going on with Michael?" I push.

"Barbs, I'm under gossip lockdown, I'm afraid," he replies, frowning. Great. So there is something occurring I'm not going to like.

"You should go back down to the party. Your fans will wonder where you are." It sounds mean, but if he's not going to tell me anything, then I'd rather be alone.

"Hey, you have fans too. You're the guest of honour, and you're not there either."

I shrug, not knowing how to get rid of him.

"Come on. I'll get you a drink, and then you owe me a dance," he prods, moving to stand up. Lowering his hand for me to grab hold of, I do so reluctantly.

"I don't owe you anything."

"Oh, yes, you do."

"What's that supposed to mean?" I huff, pulling my hand out of his grasp.

"It means you don't own a fucking Prius 'cause I dragged my ass down there to see you. Just trust me. Have a drink, a dance. You know, fun, and don't be worrying about the future. It always works out in the end," he declares, taking my hand back in his.

He hadn't said anything specific, but I want to trust him enough to tell me if something is going to be bad. I let him guide me back to the bar and begin downing the shots shoved in front of us.

"How about that dance now, Barbie?"

He doesn't give me a choice. He pulls me to the makeshift dance floor and pulls me into his arms.

The song is slow, and I relax against him. It's a lot quieter in the clubhouse now. It's late, and people are either drunk and passed out, or off somewhere with their old ladies or one of the club whores. They might not behave in a gentlemanly way, but I can't imagine my life without these men being a part of it.

The clubhouse hasn't changed at all. The bar still runs along the far wall where the stairs to the dorm rooms are housed on the second floor. The huge Lost Souls fabric badge is still hanging, covering half of one of the walls, and pictures of Harley Davidsons cover the wall space that's left. Three pool tables had been pushed around to make space for the dance floor, and reclining chairs and couches are littered about.

The only difference since the last time I was here is Cas standing at the bottom of the dorm stairs, scowling at me. He must be taking a break from his fuck fest, with a cigarette hanging from his mouth and his jeans hanging low. With his bare chest slightly covered by his cut, he truly is a painfully, beautiful sight. Closing my eyes to him, I turn and bury my face into Sparky's chest. Remembering what he said about not having to worry about tomorrow, I begin to relax further, and before I know it, the music is being turned down. We've danced for what feels like hours, and my feet are now killing me.

Ever the big brother, Sparky walks me to my uncle's house and makes sure I'm inside before he turns and walks away.

# 2

## Alannah

It could be the Tequila still lingering in my system, or it could be the impending "talk" with Michael I have later today that has me feeling like I'm going to throw up. For the first time in my life, I wish I had a normal family, where coming home didn't hold so many different outcomes.

The only guarantee in my life today is the fact that the heat is already stifling, as expected. I throw back the covers and slide out of bed. Choosing a pair short shorts, a tank top, and underwear, I head toward the bathroom to get ready for the day.

Thirty minutes later, I'm making my way downstairs to the kitchen when I hear my Aunt Kitty talking to Michael. They hush as I enter the room and join him at the table. Their silence only causes my nausea to worsen.

"After you've eaten, meet me in my office and we'll talk,"

he announces. Rising from the table, he immediately heads for the door.

Once we hear it slam shut, my aunt shoots across the kitchen.

Her flaming red hair falls around my face and her thin, yet very strong arms envelope me in a bone-crushing hug. She isn't a big woman, but I swear she has the strength of a man three times her size.

I laugh nervously and hug her back. It dawns on me that she would know what my uncle has in store for me, but as a loyal old lady, she wouldn't open her mouth. Her reaction, though, has convinced me that I won't like what my uncle has to say.

I barely touch my eggs and bacon, deciding to get this over and done with.

"I'll see you later, Kitty!" I call out, escaping out the door before she can reply.

It's still pretty early as I cross the compound to the clubhouse where my uncle's office is. Inside, it wreaks of booze, smoke, and women. A couple of prospects are on cleaning duty, and by the looks on their faces, they aren't happy about it. But being prospects, they get assigned all the grunt work.

Cas is coming out of the office as I'm walking down the hall. I hate my body for reacting to the sight of him in his jeans and black tee, showing off the tattoos snaking up and down his arms. Sticking to my promise of ignoring him, I move to the side and wait for him to pass, but instead of continuing on, he stops and stares at me.

"Hey, you're the one who said to stay out of your way, so

can you do me the same courtesy? I need to go in there." Gesturing to the office door, I'm surprised at how firm my words sound.

He blinks and moves to the side, staying there until I knock, waiting for permission to enter. When my uncle calls me in, I don't look back and shut the door behind me.

"Hey, darlin'. Take a seat," Michael deadpans, nodding to the chair opposite his desk.

It feels like I'm back in high school, being called in to the headmaster's office instead of my uncle's.

His office isn't as large as some of the other rooms. A large wooden desk takes up most of the space, with his large chair on one side and two smaller chairs on the other. The wood panelled walls make the room darker than it should be for this time of day, with the sun shining as bright as it is. Once I'm seated, he comes around and sits on the edge of the desk. This is bad. It's the same scene as when he told me my father had died. My father was the first President of The Lost Souls MC. He always managed to give me his full attention while never abandoning his brothers or the club. In this world we live in, it's more expected to die during club business or from an accident on the road. However, my father suffered the last year of his life from testicular cancer. To this day, the pain from missing him is still raw. I long ago tired of trying to get over his death, knowing I never would. I've just learned to keep it to one side of my heart.

My uncle looks like he's trying to find the right words to tell me whatever it is he has to say. He's not a man with a wide vocabulary, but I know him well enough to know, even if he doesn't know how to tell me, his decision will be final.

"Before I say what I've got to say, I want to say how fuckin' proud of you I am. The first in our family to graduate college. Fuck, you're the first to actually go to college." He smiles at me fondly.

I only went because he gave me no choice, and while I hated every minute of it, being away from home, I'm glad I went.

"Thanks. What's this about, Uncle Mikey?" I question. The longer he stalls, the more I dread the answer.

"While you've been away, the club has been through some shit. You were safer at college than here, and now that you're back, I've made the decision to move you to our house in town. It'll keep you away from the club."

"Excuse me?" I shriek.

I know I sound like a spoilt brat, but I can't believe it. I have to leave?

I knew it was a possibility, but I never thought he would actually make it a reality.

"This life isn't for you, Alannah. You deserve so much better. The place I chose for you is in a safe location. It belongs to the club, so you needn't pay rent. I'll cover the bills for a while. You'll be fine."

"And what if I don't want to go?" I ask stubbornly.

"You have no fuckin' choice, girl. You'll do as you're told," he snaps.

"I've always done as you've asked. I went to college when I didn't want to, but I really don't want this. Please, there has to be something I can do for you around here?" I beg.

"Alannah, your father left you in my care. I'm only doing what he wanted for you. He never wanted this life for you. I let you grow up in the club because it was easier for me, but now that you're an adult, you can look after yourself," he says softly as he kneels down in front of me, taking my hands.

I knew if my father was still alive, he wouldn't push me away. He would keep me close.

"Please, Alannah. Business is getting bad around here at the moment, and I don't want you to be a part of it. Don't you understand? This is your chance to be free of the club."

As his words sink in, I want to vomit. I don't want to be free of the club. He's making this out as if it's something I want, when it couldn't be further from the truth. Then it dawns on me. People who leave can't come back.

"Are you banning me from the club?" I whisper, on the verge of tears.

"Not as such, but you won't have free rein anymore. This is for the best, Alannah. You have an hour to pack your things up. One of the prospects will help you and drive you into town."

An hour? That's all I get?

I honestly don't know what to say, so I say nothing. The look in his eyes tells me there's nothing I can say that will change his mind, and there's no point in arguing. I stare at the man who has raised me since my father died when I was six years old. His long greying hair and dark beard covers his handsome face, looking so much like my father's, but he's barely recognisable to me now. How can this be happening?

I stand slowly and walk away. If he doesn't have anything further to say, then neither do I.

I don't give him the satisfaction of slamming the door behind me, and wipe the few tears that have escaped down my cheeks. Everyone must have known what was going to happen to me. No one warned me. Not one teeny-tiny heads-up of what was to come.

Fuck everyone. I've obviously been kidding myself, believing I have a family here. Without a doubt, I know my uncle would have had this planned for a while, and when they came to collect me from college, they would've known what was in store for me. Like the worst fucking nightmare, everyone is filing into the clubhouse. Normally, they would still be in bed, but today of all days, they have to be here to witness my humiliation.

I focus my gaze on the door that leads outside and make my way toward it, but Sparky makes a beeline for me, putting his arm across the door to stop me from leaving. I keep my eyes on his bare arm, focusing on the scar that runs along one of his Lost Souls tattoos.

"Move. Please," I growl.

"Don't be like this. None of us wanted this for you," he insists, looking at everyone in the bar.

I slowly turn to see exactly who's here.

Oak, Pope, Slade, the prospects who were cleaning earlier, and a couple of club whores who had woken up with a brother. Most of them look at me, silently telling me they don't agree with this decision. Oak nurses his whiskey with an apologetic frown. The last one I come across is Cas, who's found himself a different hang-around while I was in the office.

"You knew what he was planning," I force out through gritted teeth, trying to push him out of my way. "You knew, and you told me last night not to worry."

I desperately want to scream and cry, but I won't. Not in front of them.

"I couldn't say anything. I fucking tried to get him to change his mind, but he wasn't having any of it!" he shouts back.

I believe him, and my anger deflates with his sincerity. He's as happy about this as I am.

"Doesn't matter now. I have nothing to do with this place."

"Of course you do, you just can't live here. Might not be as bad as you think."

I can tell he's trying to make light of the situation, but he hadn't heard what my uncle said.

"Do you know what that makes me feel like?" I ask angrily.

He shakes his head, but he knows.

"It makes me feel like a fucking club whore. Oh, hold on, they have more right to be here than I do," I hiss.

"Hey!" one of the whores protests.

"Shut the fuck up," someone advises her.

"Excuse me, Miss Alannah, your uncle said to remind you, you only have an hour," a prospect informs me as he walks over.

"Fuck off," I mutter. "Now move," I tell Sparky.

I don't want to fight with him, but my humiliation is getting the better of me.

"Do you want me to take you into town? The prospect can take your things in the truck."

"No. If I have no part in the club, then I don't want anything from any of you. Now please, get out of my way," I beg. I know it's not fair, that I'm being a real bitch, but he won't let me leave, and the whole scene is utterly embarrassing.

He grabs me by both wrists and pulls me into him.

"Don't be so fucking stupid, Barbie. We're still your family," he warns.

"I don't want anything." I narrow my eyes and add, "And I've told you, don't call me Barbie."

Girls play with Barbie dolls when they're young, and that's acceptable. Me, the MC princess, owned every Barbie doll available, and with natural blonde hair of my own, I was given that nickname.

It was cute when I was six, but now, it's insulting.

"Let her go."

Everyone turns to see Cas moving toward us. Sparky doesn't want to let me go, but he can't refuse his Vice President's order. Sparky reluctantly releases me, but doesn't move out of my way.

"Prospect, go and pack her things and bring the truck around. Force her in if you have to," he orders him.

"I'll pack myself. I'm not having no fucking prospect touch my things," I snap.

Cas ignores me and nods for the prospect to follow his orders. As he goes to pass me, I stand in his way. I don't know this prospect, but he looks like he hasn't bathed in months, and this is the man my uncle and former club wants to help me? Un-fucking-believable.

"If you force me in that truck, I'll knock you upside your fucking head all the way to where you're forcing me to go."

I'm not usually violent by nature, but as humiliated as I feel, I just want to get out of here and disappear.

The prospect starts to squirm, looking frantically between his VP and me. It would be comical if I wasn't so mad.

He'll never make the cut if he can't deliver one girl to a house half an hour away. Pathetic.

"Fucking hell, woman. Can't you for once do as you're told?" Cas groans.

"Screw you. First of all, I'm trying to leave. Second, you don't get to talk to me," I tell him, pointing my finger in his direction.

Before I know it, he crosses the distance between us and throws me over his shoulder, yelling for the prospect to follow him.

I'm an outcast, and I'm being treated as such. But it doesn't stop me from fighting him all the way to the house. He carries me up the stairs, opening doors until he finds my room and throws me on my bed.

"Pack your shit," he bellows and leaves.

I can't help it. I break down and cry. I can't believe what just happened. Aunt Kitty comes in and holds me, soothing me in her arms.

"I'm so sorry this happened, baby," she whispers in my ear, over and over.

"Why?" I cry, sobbing against her shoulder.

"I don't know. Bad things have been happening you don't know about. I trust your uncle is doing what he believes is for the best."

I cry in her arms for a few more minutes before she pulls away and begins helping me pack.

"I don't want the prospect to drive me. Can you call me a cab?"

"Michael won't like it. Just take the ride and ignore the prospect," she urges.

I back down and start packing. For some reason, I thought I would only need some clothes and my few measly possessions I couldn't live without, until I see the stack of cardboard boxes piled up in the corner. This is it. He expects me to take everything, wipe away all traces of me ever being here.

~

With two minutes to spare out of my one-hour time limit, the prospect hauls out the last box and puts it into the back of the truck before jumping behind the wheel.

I share one last hug with Kitty and climb into the passenger seat. The drive through and out of the compound is eerily quiet, and I thank God for that. At least there's no one around to see my degrading departure.

After ten minutes on the road, something feels wrong.

"Where are you taking me? I was told I was going into town."

"Last minute change. I was told to take you to the cabin," is all he says. Probably afraid I'll hit him upside the head as promised.

I used to love going to the cabin when I was younger, but now it feels like a punishment.

I'd been looking so forward to coming home, and now I don't have one, no family. And to top it off, I'm going to be stuck in the middle of nowhere, and on my own.

Forty-five minutes later, the truck stops outside the cabin, and the prospect comes around and opens my door. He's beginning to get on my good side, where I don't want him to be. I want to be pissed at everyone who had a part in ousting me from the club.

"Why don't you go in, Miss Alannah, and I'll bring your stuff inside." He smiles, and it's a nice smile, with straight, white teeth.

"It's okay, I can help you," I offer.

"No! I'll do it. I was told you weren't to lift anything," he exclaims, sounding mortified that he wouldn't be able to do as he was instructed.

I step back, holding my hands up in surrender.

"Okay, then, I'll make us a drink," I laugh.

He visually relaxes, and begins hauling boxes inside.

Once he's on a roll, it doesn't take long before I have boxes piled high in the living room. I'm instructed to write a list of everything I need, and looking around the kitchen, I see I need a lot. There's no food or cleaning supplies, and for some reason, there aren't any plates.

The prospect takes the list and tells me he'll be back by nightfall with the goods.

I don't want to be on my own. I do everything I can think of to entice him to stay longer, but he's adamant that he has a job to do.

Sighing loudly to myself, I look around the cabin. I thought life couldn't get any worse.

Cas

I can't work out if I'm happy she's gone or miserable. I won't see her around the place, even though I could never get close to her.

She looked broken when she came out of Michael's office. Everything was so fucked-up, I couldn't think straight. The decision to throw her over my shoulder was a selfish one. I wanted to feel her against me. All she saw was a form of removal, but the few minutes it took to get her to Michael's house was heaven to me. My hands gripping her soft skin, I wanted more, and not in a one-way act. It took all my willpower not to slide my hands up to her ass.

Always having to choose the club over everything used to never be a problem. The club won each and every time, but when it came to Alannah, choices were becoming a battle.

I didn't trust myself to stay and make sure she packed. Her sprawled out on her bed was giving me ideas I couldn't afford to have. I had to hate her to make it easier to stay away from her, but holy shit, it was fucking hard, and so was my cock—for her.

I took straight off and near enough ran to my dorm room, jumped in the shower, and stayed there long enough for Alannah to leave, and then stayed in my room long after.

The atmosphere is at an all-time low when I finally return to my brothers. It's as if someone has died and they're in mourning.

Oak hasn't moved from the bar. I think about joining him, until he abruptly gets up and leaves.

Sparky is in the corner with the prospect who was given the job of escorting Alannah to the house in town. Sparky isn't looking too happy about something, so I find a spot at the bar that will get me close enough to hear what's going on.

"What do you mean she's not fucking there?" Sparky snaps.

I can see he's losing his patience.

"Boss man told me to take her to the cabin and come back to get whatever she needs."

"Why's she at the cabin?"

The prospect shrugs. "Don't have a clue. I was told to take her there, and I did."

Something about this doesn't sit well. Michael's been making decisions without involving the club lately, and I'm sure he's been keeping secrets. Why make it known she was going to be staying at the house in town, and then have her taken to the cabin? She's now in a secluded area, on her own, while the club is in one of the worst situations we've faced in years with the Raging Riders up our asses. She's like a sitting duck out there. I'm sure Michael hasn't warned her of the dangers she could be facing. Alannah has never been a pushover, and I wouldn't underestimate her if she had to defend herself by any means necessary, but the Raging Riders will do anything to destroy our club. They've been trying to take us out for the last two years—without much luck—and they're getting nastier in their attacks. If they knew of her whereabouts, then a single prospect guarding her wouldn't be enough to save her.

"What have you been told to do after you deliver her things to the cabin?"

I listen intently.

"I have to report to Michael," he mumbles, seeming

uncomfortable in relaying the information to Sparky. "Look, man, I have to go. She'll be wondering where I am. She didn't want me to leave in the first place." He then quickly adds, "She's fine. I just don't think she liked being on her own." Seeing Sparky is about to burst with anger, I jump into the conversation.

"Hey, man, why don't I follow him and make sure she's secure?" Not that I need permission. "Then, when I get back, we'll find out what the fuck is going on."

"Something's going on, Cas. I have a bad feeling about this. It was strange enough he made her go, but to stick her at the cabin?" he remarks, looking confused.

I agree with him. I slap his shoulder as I pass and make my way to my bike.

I follow closely behind the prospect's truck, keeping my eyes everywhere.

I've been to the cabin a few times. It's impressive in size, and way too big for one girl on her own in my opinion. The outside needs attention. The bushes and trees are beginning to take over, and for miles around, there's not another house in sight.

Alannah is perched on the steps, waiting, her smile disappearing when she sees me riding behind. It's not replaced with the usual repulsion I've come to expect from her, but more like confusion.

I nod to the prospect to start unloading the truck. While I wait for him to finish and leave, I pull a cigarette from the pack in my pocket and light up, inhaling deeply.

I don't have a clue what I'm doing here. One of the brothers could have easily checked on her. I should've stayed at the clubhouse, as there wasn't any reasonable explanation for me being here, apart from my selfish need to see her.

She stays out of sight in the house with the prospect, no doubt hiding from me, trying to figure out why I'm here.

Just as I'm about to light another cigarette, the prospect comes walking out. I nod for him to join me.

"You going back to the clubhouse?"

"Yeah. Gotta see Michael."

"What's he got you doing?" I ask, none too kindly. By the way his eye twitches, I know he's not meant to say anything.

"Nothin'. I gotta go see him now." He quickly jogs off to his truck.

Frowning slightly, I head inside and find her in the kitchen, cleaning the fridge. She sees me leaning against the doorframe, and returns to her task.

"What are you doing here?" she asks.

Good question.

"I came to make sure you're okay."

She stands abruptly and narrows her eyes at me.

"I'm just peachy. Now you can leave."

Her mouth is making me hard again. I need to have her. I mentally punch myself in the head. I should turn and walk away, seeing as she's more than fine. I should definitely go. Instead, two stupid fucking words leave my mouth.

"I'm sorry," I croak out, barely loud enough for her to hear. Maybe I want her to hear it, maybe not, but I am sorry.

"There's nothing to be sorry for," she replies, continuing to keep her back to me.

I wasn't planning on ever talking about this with her. All

plans of ignoring her and staying well away from her completely evaporated when she came home from college.

Memories from last summer surface. The girl I couldn't stay away from. The way she smiled, the sound of her laugh, the thought of her in my bed and never leaving. She was the first girl I wanted to be with properly, to make her mine and no one else's. There were no comparisons to the other girls around the club or around town.

"Of course there fucking is. I know I hurt you."

"I was hurt, but I got over it," she snaps, slamming the fridge door shut.

I move closer to her. I know she's still hurt. Otherwise, she wouldn't have turned away from me when we picked her up on the college campus.

"I didn't."

She looks genuinely confused. "I didn't get over it," I clarify.

"If I remember rightly, you were under it," she mutters sarcastically.

"Don't," I warn.

"I told you, you don't get to talk to me."

"I'll do what the fuck I like. You going to stop me?" I ask, stepping closer.

Before she can argue back, I slam my lips onto hers. We'd shared a few kisses last summer, but my memory hadn't recalled just how good her lips felt against mine.

She protests at first, but soon melts against me. I deepen the kiss, forcing her lips open with my tongue. Finally fisting my hand in her hair, I keep her close to me. I push my luck when I hear her groan into my mouth and slam her up against the wall, pulling her legs up and around my waist. She tightens her grip and fists my hair.

I want her now. I'm wrestling to get her top off when she begins pulling away.

"I can't do this."

I continue to kiss down her neck, and she surrenders for a few seconds before pushing me away as hard as she can. I stumble back as she darts across the room, as far from me as she can possibly get.

"You should go," she pants, turning away from me.

"Why?"

If I leave now, I won't be able to think of anything else all fucking night, and the need to release myself would be inside of some dirty whore. But I don't want that anymore. All I want is Alannah.

"Because... I shouldn't have done that. I hate you!" Turning back toward me, she gives me her best glare yet. Anyone else might find it intimidating, as I can tell she means it, but it only turns me on. The way her cheeks redden, her rapid breathing increases, and the glaze sweeping across her eyes. It all has me nearly falling to my knees.

"You want me," I counter.

She roars with laughter.

"Once, I did, but now I just hate you."

I edge closer to her, maintaining eye contact. I'm having her tonight, and she's having me. It should have happened a long time ago. It's been a very long time in the making.

"Take your hate out on me. Show me how much you hate me. Show me how much I hurt you."

"W–What? You're crazy," she stammers, backing away from me.

"And I'll show you how much I've always wanted you, and how fucking sorry I am. I'll make you forget everything," I tell her, closing the distance between us again.

I hold back, waiting for her to take the next step. As soon as I see her relenting, I can't stop myself. I lean in and take her mouth again. It doesn't take long before she's kissing me back, dragging my cut over my shoulders and letting it fall to the floor. My tee is ripped over my head and discarded before I can blink.

A year. That's how long I've waited for this, and I wasn't going to wait a second longer. I scoop her up in my arms and take her upstairs. For the second time today, I throw her on the bed, but this time, I'm not walking away.

She climbs on all fours, crawls across the bed and latches onto my belt, pulling me forward. I frown at how expertly and swiftly she has it undone and my jeans down. She'd shyly admitted to me last year she was a virgin and was embarrassed by it, but I found it hot, knowing that I would be the first and only dick inside of her, because she sure as shit wouldn't have been fucking anyone else while I was around.

Before I can read too much into it, she has my dick in her mouth, sucking it like a goddamn lollipop. Grabbing her hair in both hands, I push deeper into her mouth, and she fucking takes it like a pro.

Less than a minute in her mouth and I'm about to blow my load straight down her throat, but I'm not ready to finish yet—not even close. Reaching over her to pull her legs out from underneath her is a mistake, because she fucking bites down on my cock.

"What the fuck, woman?" I snap, pulling away from her.

"You told me to show you how much I hate you."

"Oh, you're gonna pay for that."

"So are you."

Staying where she is on the bed, she shimmies out of her shorts, leaving just her panties on and smiles wickedly before opening her legs as wide as she can, trailing her clit with her finger. The sight of her wetness showing through is hot as hell. Fuck, I have to be inside her.

In the next moment, I'm on top of her, ripping her panties to the side and sliding my cock inside her. Tight, oh so fucking tight, every thrust had her screaming.

"Scream my name, baby," I growl.

"Fuck off," she yells out defiantly.

I dig my hips into her thigh, and she opens her legs even wider, begging for more as she grinds against me, tightening around my cock every time she moves. I'm not going to last much longer.

"Fucking scream for me, baby."

"Fuck you."

"You're fucking me," I groan close to her ear. She proceeds to get the better of me, and before I know it, she has me flipped over and is on top of me.

"I hate you," she groans quietly, digging her nails in my thighs as she leans back, thrusting her chest out as she starts to ride me.

For the first time in my life, I can do nothing but lie there and take what this fucking goddess is giving me. I can feel her clenching around me, reaching her climax. When she falls forward against my chest, I take over. Crushing her against me, I pound into her until she cries out a final time, and we explode together.

## Alannah

*This is what it should have been like a year ago*, I think to myself, still slumped across Cas's chest. Then, what he did shoots to the forefront of my mind, but I'm still immobilised from the most intense orgasm I've ever had to do nothing but let the tears fall onto his chest. I hate myself for not keeping him away and making him leave. I hate myself for responding to his touch. And most of all, I hate myself for loving every second of being with him. I'm pathetic. My second night back and I'm already in his arms.

He gently rolls me off of him, leaves the room, and quickly returns with a washcloth. It's such an intimate act for him to clean me up afterward. How can he be so gentle now when I know how cruel he can be?

I'm hit suddenly with the realisation that we didn't use a condom. I'm on birth control, but with his numerous conquests, I can't trust that he's clean. Shit! This just gets better and better.

"I'm so sorry, Lana," he whispers, over and over, trailing soft kisses across my stomach.

I can't hear his apologies anymore. I push his head away and roll onto my side, away from him.

"Don't do this, baby. I know you hate me for what I did, but there's a whole lot of shit you don't know."

Him making excuses makes me feel worse. I can't look at him. Everything we shared was ruined when he went to bed with one of the club sluts. I know the kind of life the club leads, with different women each night, even if they have old ladies waiting at home for them. Violence and deception. None of that mattered to me, because I thought Cas was different. Of course, I knew he wasn't an angel, but for an entire summer, he was more than an angel to me. He was a god.

Tonight was nothing but closure. I'll never have to wonder what that night would have been like if it had played out differently.

"I don't want to know. What's done is done. It doesn't matter now."

"It matters to me—*you* matter to me," he declares.

I hear the sincerity in his voice, but I also heard it last year, and look how that ended up. I have no club, and no college to run away to. I'm all on my own now. And even if I could trust him, there's no way this would work. From the minute my uncle sent me here, we were worlds apart.

"I shouldn't matter to you, because tonight meant nothing. Go back to your club and leave me alone," I beg.

The sooner he leaves, the sooner I can try to forget about him.

"Tonight meant everything, and you fucking know it," he hisses. "And if you think I'm leaving you alone, you're fucking wrong."

"I don't care anymore. You do what you've got to do, and I'll do what I've got to do."

"What the fuck is that supposed to mean?" he snaps angrily.

I've had enough now. Sitting up, I get in his face.

"It means fuck off! You think because we fucked tonight, I'm just going to forget everything?" I shout, losing my temper. "You're never going to change. You're the club, and I'm not anymore. You got what you wanted, so just get out!"

"I'm going to find out what's going on, Lana. I'm going to fix this for you," he promises.

"If that's what eases your guilt, whatever."

I'm physically and emotionally exhausted. After being kicked out of the club and tonight's escapades, I have nothing left.

I think our stare off is never going to end until he suddenly crushes his lips against mine. It's a hard, fast kiss, and then he's sliding out of the bed and back into his jeans.

Turning as he fastens his belt buckle, he proclaims,

"It's never over between us."

He's at the door when I call out, "It's never going to begin!"

"It just did!" he shouts back.

He laughs as he runs down the stairs and out the door, and all I can do is sit here, frozen, until I hear the rumble of his bike fade into the distance.

No longer having the energy for anything, not even to think, I fall back and curl around the pillow. I'm asleep within seconds.

# 3

## Alannah

The morning comes around too fast. Stretching my legs out, I feel stiff and slightly sore from the previous night. Normally, I'm not one for laying around in bed in the mornings, but today, I can't find a single reason to get up. Dark clouds are moving across the sky as I look out of the window. Perfect weather for my mood.

Clattering and banging from downstairs has me jumping out of bed. I search the drawers in the room and find an oversized T-shirt and throw it over my head. *Maybe I should have more self-preservation*, I think as I run down the stairs, heading straight for the kitchen where I find Sparky having an argument with the coffee maker. Laughing to myself, I cross the room and take over.

"Morning, Barbs. I was wondering when you were going to show your face," he chuckles.

I choose to ignore his "Barbie" jibe and reach for the mugs.

"What are you doing here?" I still haven't forgiven him for lying to me.

"I followed the prospect up. He's been posted to watch over you," he says simply.

And just like all other times we argue, a simple conversation puts us back on track in our friendship.

"Why?"

"Because your uncle decided he needed to be here. Shit's getting crazy out there, and he wanted to make sure you're safe," he explains, leaning against the countertop.

"I don't know why he's bothering. If I was in any danger, surely I would be at the compound instead of here."

"My thoughts exactly. Anyway, you coming to the party tomorrow night? Everyone's been asking about you."

His quick change of subject isn't lost on me, but I don't push further. I know the need-to-know basis is in play.

"I don't know. There's so much to do around here. Maybe next week... that's if I'm allowed," I mumble, taking my coffee out onto the deck.

He raises his eyebrow at me, telling me not to be stupid.

The clubhouse on a Saturday night is party time. All the guys unleash their previous week's work, run-ins, and stresses on alcohol and women. Once I was old enough, I was allowed to attend, and I didn't care about the sex side of it. It was well known I wasn't to be touched by anyone, and when I left the compound to go shopping or wherever, I would always have someone watching me, so losing my virginity was one of the hardest tasks I faced. It wasn't until after Cas humiliated me that I lost my virginity to a guy at college. At the parties, I liked to drink, dance, let loose, and have a laugh.

Sparky follows me outside and we sit, chatting over our coffees until his cell beeps and he has to go.

I walk him out to his bike and sigh.

"I wish life could go back to how it used to be," I muse.

Jealous of him clipping his helmet in place and about to ride his beast of a machine away from here, I hold myself tight and ignore the need to ride with him like old times. There's never been any attraction between Sparky and I, only a sibling type of relationship. Being older than me, he took on the big brother role and has never let me down.

"Life's always changing, Barbs. Sometimes it isn't fair, but the majority of the time, it all works out in the end."

Before I spout off that he's spewing a load of bullshit, I nod and hug him goodbye instead.

"I'll come by tomorrow. Let me know if you need anything, okay?"

"Okay."

I feel like a tiny part of me dies every time someone leaves me here. Why is my uncle doing this to me? And why do I need a guard?

Completely ignoring the prospect's presence on the porch chair, I go inside and slam the door shut behind me.

Target for today: attack the kitchen with bleach and scrub it clean.

~

Scrubbing and dusting until four this morning, the kitchen

was as clean as it was ever going to get. In the predawn light, the walls look washed out, and in dire need of makeover. So, after five hours of sleep, I get washed and dressed, and instruct the prospect to drive me into town so I can buy some paint. It looks like I'm here for the foreseeable future, so I might as well make it as homely as I can for myself.

The prospect is more help than I thought he would be. So far, he's stayed out of my way. He hasn't even been in the house to use the bathroom. During our trip to the hardware store, he maintained a five-foot distance behind me, and after a half hour of me debating on what paint I needed, he offered his input. In the end, I told him what colour I wanted, and he went off and got everything I would need. Another highlight of the trip was, he told me the club would pay.

I expected him to return to his guarding post on the porch when we were finished, but he looked indecisive about something.

"What's up, bodyguard?" I ask.

"No offence, but do you need me to help?"

I laugh. He's not as tall as some of the other brothers, but his stocky build with his strong jawline enhances a kick-ass look about him. His hair is in between growing out. Most prospects start with short hairstyles, and usually by the time they make the cut, their hair has reached their shoulders. Sparky is the only biker in the mother chapter that keeps his hair short.

"Yes."

We work mostly in silence, apart from when I need his assistance, and he'll reply with short, clipped answers. He's not rude about it. I can tell he's just staying in his place. He's here to guard me, not to socialise. I suppose my uncle would have made that crystal clear to him.

Fed up with calling him prospect, I ask for his real name.

"Billy."

"Well, Billy." I smile. "Thank you for your help. I guess I'm pretty shitty at this," I say, nodding toward the one tiny wall I'm attempting to paint.

"You're not that bad. It takes practice. If you get the urge to decorate the entire house, you'll end up a pro," he chuckles.

What he says triggers something in me. It's daunting to think I'll be here for a long time, long enough to redecorate.

"Can you tell me why Michael put you here?" If anyone would know, surely he would.

"I'll tell you what I told Sparky and Cas. I was told to keep an eye on you, that's all." He seems irritated with having to explain himself again. What intrigues me, though, is that Sparky, and mostly Cas, are questioning my uncle as well. I wouldn't expect any less from Sparky, but why would Cas be so interested?

Maybe I should go to the party tonight, try and find out what's going on. It wouldn't hurt to show my face and see if anything is out of place. Which at a biker's club, it would be hard to pinpoint.

"How do you fancy blowing this off and going back to the club? You can have a break from babysitting me."

"Sounds good to me. I'll pack this lot away while you go and get changed," he offers.

It occurs to me as I'm getting ready to shower that it's highly likely Cas will be there tonight, and while I want nothing to do with him, I still want to look hot and show him what he'll never have again.

Smiling to myself, I choose my shortest skirt and leather halter neck top before jumping into the shower.

## Cas

Sparky was nowhere to be found when I got back last night. After spending time with Alannah, I'm making it a priority to find out what Michael is up to. There had to be a reason why he forced her out of the club, and then into the cabin instead of the townhouse.

Michael has always been a fast thinking and precise man. It's what makes him the great leader he is. There's been a few times he's made decisions without involving the club, and they always worked out. The club always benefits financially, and whatever the deal, it's cemented our reputation further so that no other club takes advantage.

I've never questioned his motives before. I've trusted him and been loyal to him since I was seventeen years old. Kicked out of high school and finding myself in trouble at every opportunity, moving from foster home to foster home, he gave me a proper home and a family within the club. He gave me a job in the garage and trained me to work on the cars and bikes. I was only a prospect for three months before I was patched in on my eighteenth birthday. Usually, it's about a year on probation minimum, proving yourself worthy of wearing the cut.

Coming out of the garage, I glimpse Sparky walking toward the clubhouse. I jog over and pull him to the side.

"Where did you get to last night? I looked around for you, but left when I saw your bike wasn't here," he says.

"I went to the cabin like I said I would, then went for a ride."

"So what the fuck's going on, VP?"

"I don't know," I tell him honestly. "I want to know what you think."

"All I know is, this shit with the Raging Riders is spiraling out of control, and I think Michael will do anything to bring them down."

"Do you think Alannah has any part in this?" I ask, praying he can settle my growing fears.

"Honestly, if she does, then I don't think she has any knowledge of it, which puts her in more danger."

His fears are the same as mine. If he's making decisions using women, then it puts us all in danger.

I swing around and punch the wall. The pain shooting up my arm takes the edge off of wanting to find our President and find out the truth with violence.

I hate that I feel like this toward him. There's nothing worse in a club than having doubts about a fellow brother, but more so when it's the President.

"What the fuck are we gonna do?"

"All we can do is keep our eyes open and check in with Alannah as much as we can, without bringing attention to ourselves."

"If he's using her in any way, I'll fucking kill him," I warn, meaning it.

"You need to cool down, brother," he snaps, pulling me farther away from the clubhouse.

"We need to be smart about this. We know fucking nothing. You go in there accusing Michael without proof, he'll cover his tracks and we'll never find out what the fuck is going on."

He speaks sense. Even through my anger, I know he's right, but the urge to jump straight in with fists first, questions later, is overwhelming.

"Has something happened between you and Barbie I need to know about?" he inquires, narrowing his eyes.

I don't want to lie to a brother, but technically, I'm not. He doesn't need to know about the other night.

"No. I just want to make sure she's protected, and in my opinion, one prospect isn't enough protection. Not when it comes to her."

From his look, I know he doesn't believe me, but he drops it. He's just as worried as I am. Alannah is like a sister to him, and from past experience, I know he'll go to any lengths to make sure she doesn't get hurt.

Both our phones beep at the same time, alerting us to a message. It's from Slade.

"A meeting on a Saturday night? What the fuck is going on now?" Sparky groans.

"Let's find out," I reply, beginning to walk away.

"Hold up," he calls out, catching up and stepping in front of me. "Keep your cool in there. If we act like nothing's up, then he might slip up."

"Fine. Have you seen her today?"

"I swung by but she wasn't there. Apparently, the prospect

took her into town today because she wanted to do some redecorating, so I'll go by again tomorrow."

"Is she coming by tonight?"

"She said no. Come on, we need to get in there," he tells me, turning away.

~

The room at the back of the clubhouse is open. Everyone, apart from Sparky and I, are already seated around the table. Sparky follows me in and closes the doors behind us. The whole lot of them look as confused as we do. Only Michael sits stone-faced at the head of the table.

We take our places, Sparky at my side and me at Michael's. Until I know what's going on, I can't trust him, and that hurts.

"I called you all here because we have a situation," he starts, taking a deep breath before continuing. "A couple of hours ago, Micky's body was found next to his bike, which has been stripped. Looks like he was dumped after being tortured."

The table erupts into chaos. Micky was a Lost Souls original who went nomad a few years back when he lost his wife to cancer. He stopped by every few months, stayed a couple of days, then returned to the road.

Michael brings the table to order and carries on, apparently not finished.

"I'm having photos sent through, but according to Lincoln, Micky was found with the word 'RAT' carved into his forehead," he adds, frowning. Lincoln is the President of our supporting club, the Devil's Bastards.

Shit!

"No way would Micky rat. It's a motherfuckin' lie!" Oak roars, banging his fist on the table.

Once again, the table is in chaos, everyone shouting over one another. I sit there, stunned, trying to work out what the fuck is going on. Shit's getting crazier every day.

"Quiet!" Michael stands, resting his hands on the table. "I don't believe it any more than all of you that Micky would turn against us, but we have to act as if he did." That gets everyone's attention.

"He was here last week when we were discussing the run up north scheduled for Monday. We can't afford to dismiss the possibility they might have that information, just to be on the safe side."

"The only side we should be on is Micky's. We should be planning revenge, not carrying on with business," Oak disputes.

"Until we know what the fuck happened, we stick to the original plan."

Michael is calm—too calm. He has a plan of action already in mind, and retribution isn't going to be pretty.

"What the fuck do you propose we do, then?" Sparky prods.

"We call in brothers from our northern chapter and make two runs. Instead of the real run on Monday, we do a fake run. If Micky did talk and they show up, we can finally take them out, then move the real delivery to a different day with a new route."

My brothers look happy with this plan. None of us could believe Micky would hurt the club this way, but if it was a set up, then we'd finally have our revenge for every attack the Raging Riders have placed on us over the last few years.

"It's the only fuckin' way we can get these motherfuckers'. Anyone against?"

Every head around the table shakes. No one's against it. This type of plan is what we've been waiting for. If this plan goes in our favor, then it means a brother went against us. If they don't show up, it's cool, a brother didn't rat, but then we're no closer to the Raging Riders. It's kind of a win-lose situation either way.

"Good. Be back here tomorrow night at seven and we'll go over the details. Now, let's go and drink to our lost brother."

The atmosphere is split between the loss of Micky, the possibility he turned against the club, and the high of an impending fight. No matter who was feeling what, there's no doubt there wouldn't be any sober brothers by the end of the night.

As each brother leaves the room, I remain in my seat. When Michael sees this, he stays behind as well and sits in his chair.

"What's on your mind, VP?" he asks, pulling out his pack of cigarettes.

He takes one out and pushes the pack toward me. I take one and light up, inhaling deeply, before coming straight out with what I want to know.

"Does Alannah have anything to do with all this?"

He blows out a long stream of smoke and closes his eyes, tiredness and old age showing on his face.

"What's this really about, Cas?"

"I just want to know. Is there any more to it where Alannah is concerned?"

"I'm only going to say this once more. Alannah won't live this life. Her father didn't want her around the club, and as his blood brother, I'll honour his wish and give her everything I can to help her." He pauses before adding, "This shouldn't be your concern."

I sit there calmly, reining in my temper. I don't believe that's what Mark would've wanted for his daughter from everything I've heard about him from the old timers. I've never picked up any signs from them he had another agenda for her, but the feeling in the pit of my stomach still remains, and it's never failed me yet.

"You're right. I don't know what I was thinking," I say, rising out of my chair.

"I appreciate your concern, but it isn't needed where Alannah is concerned. Stay away from her, Cas," he warns once again. "Now, come on. Let's go and join the others."

We leave the room and enter the clubhouse to loud music, and everyone milling around outside by the open fire.

As soon as I sit down at one of the picnic tables with everyone else, Michael as good as throws one of the club whores on my lap. I catch the brief look in his eyes and know exactly what he's doing. He's testing me. So, I play along and keep the girl where she is, readjusting her a bit so she's not on my dick. All I can think is, thank God Alannah isn't here tonight. Aware of Michael's eyes on us, I rest my hand on the girl's bare thigh. My first thought is of the contrast between her coarse skin compared to Alannah's smooth, silky thighs.

As the conversation rolls from one memory of Micky to another, I keep up the pretense of showing an interest in the girl on my lap, but as soon as Michael leaves, I'm gone.

I'm caught up in calculating how long it will take me to get to my bike and be at the cabin when a fight breaks out, which isn't uncommon around here. Give it an hour, and the two involved will be laughing and speaking like nothing had happened. That's what I love about being a part of this club—the bond we share.

The fight clears a path, as everyone is making room for the brawling brothers, and Alannah appears on the other side. I'm not fucking this girl, but from the look on Alannah's face, I might as well be. Michael is watching—always fucking watching—so I have to play along, acting as if it's just her being jealous and emotional. By the time I look back to where she was standing, she's gone.

Fuck.

Clenching and unclenching my fists isn't enough to drown out my anger at the situation. There's no way I'm getting in that cabin now.

Without being obvious, I remove the girl from my lap and decide to go in search of a drink. On second thought, I grab the girl and pull her with me.

Making my way back into the clubhouse, I see Alannah by the bar with the prospect getting their drinks. He disappears, and I wait until I see him go to the bathroom to approach.

Before I can get rid of the girl holding my hand in an iron grip and casually visit the bar myself to explain to Alannah what's going on, a guy, one I haven't seen before, makes a beeline for her. I can't say I blame him. The way her short skirt is riding higher up her thighs every time she leans on the bar is hard not to notice. He probably thinks all his Christmas's have come at once. Well, until I make it clear to him to fuck off and never go near her again. She catches my eye and quickly turns her back to me, laughing at something he says, and rests her hand against his chest. I know she's only doing it to get a rise out of me, and it fucking works. Where the hell is Sparky to sort this shit out?

I see Michael come in behind us and get caught up in a conversation with Oak by one of the pool tables. I have to play this right. Otherwise, I'll be going against Michael's orders, and everyone here tonight will be witness to it.

Looking back to Alannah, I see the prospect still isn't back, and the guy who has joined her is groping her ass. Becoming angry that she's allowing him to touch her, I keep hold of the girl's hand and walk over to the bar. With my back toward the guy, I strike up a meaningless conversation with my girl, while keeping a constant ear on what they're talking about. It's the usual bullshit pick-up lines, and exaggerated girly giggle in response. It's taking everything I have in me to stop myself from ripping his face off and outright killing him right here at the bar.

"So, darlin', you got a man here?" he inquires.

"I have a lot of men here," she counters.

I know she means she has the men here wrapped around her little finger, but he takes it as her being a club slut.

"Really?"

"Yeah. You see the two guys over by the pool table? One's my uncle by blood, and the other is my uncle through the club."

"Ain't he, like, the boss man around here?" the guy questions, sounding a bit worried now.

"Yeah. He's the main man around here, I suppose."

I can't help the smirk that forms on my lips. She's playing him, and now I won't have to step in because she's doing good all on her own. If she wants to get back at me, then she wouldn't have told him who she really is.

"But, you see, they never let me have any fun, and none of them are allowed to come near me, if you know what I mean."

Fuck, she's back to flirting with him again.

"What about me? Am I allowed near you?"

"I'm not sure anyone is. They're quite protective of me," she sighs, continuing to play with him.

"But I'm fed up with their bullshit rules and lies." That was definitely for my benefit. "Hey, how about we get out of here? We could go back to my place. Fuck these guys."

She's going too far now. This guy has to disappear, and I have to tell Alannah to keep her fucking legs shut. This isn't how she normally acts, and I don't want her fucking this guy because she's pissed off at me.

Sparky and Slade stagger into the bar area. I manage to make eye contact with them and mouth that Alannah's in trouble, and they both make their way over.

"Who's this, Barbs?" Sparky asks in a friendly manner, but with authority laced underneath it.

I turn slightly so I can finally see what's happening behind my back. Alannah's face is red with anger as she glares at me, before turning her attention to my brothers.

"This is my friend, Jake...or Josh. Well, something that starts with a J. Call him J," she snickers.

"I think you should move on, J," Sparky advises, throwing his arm around the guy's shoulder.

"I don't want any trouble here." The guy looks up at Sparky, holding his hands up in a defensive gesture.

"Move on, then. This one is off-limits to every fucker here. Remember that, and you'll keep your legs in working order," Slade threatens, watching the guy sulk his way out of the bar.

I hide my satisfaction by swigging from my beer.

"You didn't have to scare him away. We were only talking."

Sparky chides, "I'm not fucking stupid, Barbie. He didn't want your mouth just for conversation."

"Don't be so disgusting to me. I can handle myself, and you'll do well to remember that the next time you get in my business, because it'll be you who gets hurt."

Slade makes a quick getaway before receiving her ire, but Sparky only laughs.

"Okay, calm down. Seriously, though, I wouldn't get in your business if the guy wasn't such a worthless piece of shit."

"Great. That leaves no one in town for me then, does it? Never mind, I shouldn't have come. I want to leave. Have you seen my bodyguard?"

"Wait here, I'll go find him."

Once Sparky has gone, I turn to face her full glare.

"That was all you, wasn't it?" she snarls, trying to keep her voice low.

"Don't know what you're talking about, babe."

"Fuck you. Don't ever do that again. Stick to your club whores and leave me the hell alone."

"This isn't what it looks like—" I start.

"It's exactly what it looks like. The only difference is it's a different whore on a different day."

I knew she would be thinking about last summer, about what I did to her. There was no way I could talk to her now and tell her the truth.

"And don't be thinking I came here for you tonight. As far I'm concerned, what happened the other night was nothing. I could fuck anyone the way I fucked you, so don't think it was anything special to me, because it wasn't."

Well, that would be a fucking slap to the face if I believed her. I lean in close to her and whisper, "You finished spewing shit to me now, babe? 'Cause there wouldn't be a man left alive in this town if they went near you. This isn't what it looks like, and if I ain't fucking you, no man is."

I lean back while keeping hold of the club girl for show to everyone else.

"Everything okay here?" Sparky comes up beside us with the prospect in tow.

"All cool here, brother." I smile, feeling good about getting my point across.

Each of us look to Alannah, who's scowling. I meant what I said. If I can't have her, no one would. She's too good for the men in this town. I might not be any better, but I trust myself to protect her and give her everything she needs.

"Are you ready? There's nothing here for me." She turns on her heels and leaves, the prospect following close behind.

No one has ever made me feel like shit the way Alannah does sometimes. With everything she's going through, it wouldn't take much more for her to never return here again.

Watching the door, hoping she'll walk back through it,

Michael catches my eye. With a smile, he nods and walks away.

Satisfied he's left the party once the door is closed, I get rid of the girl on my arm. She may think her pout looks cute, but to me, she's being childish and pathetic.

All I can think about is going to the cabin, finding Alannah, and explaining what she thought she saw. Then hopefully, taking her to bed again. Even if only to have the door slammed in my face as I explain through the wood what happened, because I can't leave her thinking anything was going to happen tonight.

I'm already at the garage before I've made the final decision to go. Wrapping the bandana around my face and clasping my helmet in place, I roll my bike out into the open.

"Where are you going?" Sparky steps in front of me, blocking my way out. I hadn't realised he'd followed me out of the bar.

"For a ride," I mumble.

"You're going to see her, aren't you?" He folds his arms across his chest. "I saw what happened earlier, and just now in the bar. You still gonna tell me fucking nothing is going on with you two?"

"I'm not gonna say anything," I say sternly, meeting his gaze.

"Have it your way, then." He relaxes his stance and takes a seat on one of the crates.

"I kept my eyes open tonight and saw more than I thought."

He has my attention now. I yank the bandana down

around my neck. Taking off my helmet, I get off the bike and wait for him to explain.

"For starters, I ain't fucking stupid. I know something's up between you and Barbie, and it's not about the shit you pulled last year. You've not been yourself since she got back, and tonight she didn't look pissed, she looked wounded."

His balled-up fists don't go unnoticed. I remember the damage they caused to my ribs last time. He's the perfect man to claim Alannah as his sister. No one can get to her through him if he doesn't like you.

I want to explain. Out of every brother here, I've always been able to tell him anything, but Alannah has always been out of bounds, and because of that, I've kept it to myself.

"What else did you see?"

"I saw Michael's face. He saw everything too."

I think back to only an hour ago when most of my attention was trained on Alannah. I thought I'd played it cool, playing my role as the loyal VP to his President's command.

"And?" I urge, wanting him to get to the fucking point.

"He was smiling. The only time I see him smile like that is when something's going his way. If he has a plan, nothing will stop him from seeing it to fruition. Barbie has more to do with this than he lets on. Whatever it is, it can't be fucking good," he finishes.

I pull out my cigarettes and take a seat beside him, pulling out one for both of us and light mine up as we sit in silence.

The bad feeling I had in my stomach explodes throughout my whole body. What the fuck are we missing?

"We have to do something," I choke out. I cough, clearing my throat, and tell him, "I can't let anything happen to her. I know what I did was wrong, but you know what would've happened otherwise…" I consider what I'm going to say next, thinking I should choose my words carefully, but I realise I don't give a fuck. I'm my own fucking man, and what I want, I'm going to have.

"I'm not being told nothing anymore. What me and Alannah had last summer wasn't what it was made out to be. My actions and love for this club tore her apart, and only I can fix that." I stand and begin pacing the garage. "This is all bullshit. Whatever Michael's not telling us, we have to assume she's in this whether we like it or not. We have to protect her, because he sure as shit isn't." I take a deep breath, trying to calm down.

"Right now, I think you're the only person who can protect her more than me. But if you go to her now, not only will she not want to see you, but Michael will put two and two together and come up with God only knows. Like I said earlier, we keep our eyes open, and if you can manage to keep them off Alannah the majority of the fucking time, you might see what the bigger picture is."

I don't like being told I can't see her, but it isn't the same as before. As much as I would love Alannah to be my world, I still had responsibilities to the club. Until we figured out what was going on, I would have to go along with Sparky.

"Call her, make sure she's okay. If I can't see her tonight, I'm seeing her tomorrow," I inform him.

"Fine, but I'll come with you. It won't look suspicious that way. Plus, she needs to be told about Micky. She loved the old fucker. She might not want you near her when she finds out."

"I'm surprised she didn't hear about him tonight."

"Looks like she had other things on her mind," he retorts, raising his eyebrow.

He's right. For some reason, none of the old-timers had any children, so when Alannah was born, they all became surrogate fathers to her, especially after her old man died. They all adopted her and loved her like their own. This was going to hit her hard, and not being at the club would be harder for her to deal with. Having Sparky there is the right move, but one day, I'll be the one to console her and no other fucker.

"Fine. But brother, when all this shit's sorted, I'll take care of her, and she'll be mine. She'll be on the back of my bike and no one else's."

He stands and walks to the door, but turns around and nods.

"I knew that was your plan. Just a heads-up, though. If she's on the back of your bike and you hurt her again, I'll beat you into the ground with your own fucking bike."

He takes another couple of steps before stopping again. "Meet me here at noon tomorrow and we'll go see your girl."

He finally walks away, and I can't stop the small smile that plays on my lips. His words are his blessing. Not that she's agreed to be my girl—yet—but she will.

One brother down, the rest of the club to go.

# 4

## Alannah

I'm angry… so fucking angry. I got no sleep last night, tossing and turning until the sun came up. All the crap he said about the other night meaning something was ludicrous.

*"It matters to me. You matter to me,"* I groan, mimicking his words. I think he believed them at the time, and like a total idiot, I wanted to trust him, to mean his words. Never have I been under any illusion what the men at the club are like, especially Cas, with his hot body and Vice President status, but growing up around the clubhouse, I saw everything. As hard as the men worked and played, some of them—not all of them, but the majority—when they fell for their women, they fell hard, and the big, badass biker turned to mush. I saw the way they looked at their women, like they were the most important people in the world. Times have changed, and in this day and age, women across the world don't need to feel

like they have to depend on a man. While I don't want to depend on anyone, I do want someone to look at me like I'm the only one they can see, like the fairy tales my Aunt Kitty used to read to me when I was little. Although, I never imagined a prince riding in on his horse. It was always a biker on his Harley. My own savior dressed in leather, and he was always a Lost Souls member, never a doubt about his loyalty to the club or to me. Last summer, I thought that was Cas. Even a couple of nights ago when I succumbed to him, I wanted to believe he meant it when he said I mattered to him. He said last night wasn't what it looked like, but all I could see in my head was him fucking her over the bar.

No, I'm not going to mope around after him. Choosing to laugh rather than cry, I get my ass out of bed. I have things to do around the cabin, and life isn't going to pass me by while his high and mighty sexiness turns up and leaves whenever he bloody well feels like it.

Walking downstairs, I hear my phone beeping, alerting me I have a message. For a brief moment, I think it could be Cas, until I remember he doesn't have my number. *Stop thinking of him.*

I find my phone, and Billy, who has already made a start on the painting, in the kitchen. The previous shade of dark red is still showing through the light cream paint I'd chosen, but you can see what the finished product will be like, and I love it. It makes the kitchen seem so much bigger, and definitely much brighter.

I pick up my phone to read the text: *Sucks to be home!* Bonnie.

She's my best friend from college. She never said much

about her home life when I asked, but I got the impression it wasn't a nice one. A couple of times she would return after school breaks, limping or trying to hide suspicious bruises on her body, and always had an excuse for them.

*I'm stuck at my uncle's cabin. Come and visit,* I text back, knowing she'll refuse.

*Can't right now. Sorry. I'll come see you soon,* she replies back.

I worried I would never see her again once we were finished with college. Just because I grew up in a biker club, doesn't mean I know anything but love from my family. If Bonnie's home life is as bad as I feel it is, then I would be there for her, even if only in text messages.

*You better. Miss you,* I quickly send.

*Miss you too. Got to go. Talk soon.*

I throw my phone to the side, not caring if any damage is caused. Bonnie is the sweetest girl I have ever met, and doesn't deserve anything bad in her life. I can't help her, though, not unless she asks me for it.

"Everything okay?" Billy asks, refilling the paint tray.

"Okay as it can be, I suppose," I mutter, thankful for his presence.

Billy had kindly told me my decorating skills were atrocious, but knew how much I wanted to help, so I was still trying to cover the red wall by the back door, which when open, would hide all my hard work.

I'm about to ask Billy why he wants to become a member of the club. I never asked before, but I know the original members set up the club purely for their love of bikes and connecting veteran backgrounds. It's not that they didn't have respect for others, they just didn't want to be a part of a lawful society. They made their own world where they lived by their own rules. The newer members craved the family they never had themselves. My uncle, and father before him, made that possible.

Just as the words are about to leave my mouth, Sparky comes strolling into the kitchen, followed by Cas. My excitement to see my friend diminishes quickly.

"Hey, Barbie. Starting to look good in here," he says, looking around the room.

"Thanks to Billy." I smile, and he smiles back before being told to leave.

I scowl at the two men. Billy has become my friend. He's in *my* house, and I hate that they have power here over him too. I can't say anything, though, because this is what Billy wants. He wouldn't have it any other way.

"To what do I owe the pleasure?"

"We want to talk to you about a couple of things." Sparky takes a seat at the table with Cas, who's already made himself comfortable. With them sitting opposite of each other, the only chair available is the one between them. I inwardly sigh until I realise it's a better position to turn my back on Cas.

Whatever they want to talk about seems important. Neither of them want to speak first, even though I'm only looking at Sparky.

"Just spit it out, Sparks," I press.

"Okay. Do you have any thoughts as to why you've been put here?" He nods around the room, meaning the cabin.

I've been asking myself the same question since I got here, and all I can think of is that my uncle turned into a Grade A jerk while I was at college.

"Not really," I lie. "You?" Maybe they've found something out.

"We don't have a fucking clue, but both of us feel something is going on that we're not aware of."

It's basically what Cas said the other night. But whatever the reason, I don't care anymore. I'm beginning to like it here. The last two times I went to the club hadn't ended well for me.

"That's why I was there last night. I wanted to see if I could find anything out. Now, I don't care. So, if that's all you came to talk about, you're wasting your time," I tell them both, only keeping my eyes in Sparky's direction.

I see the hurt flash through Sparky's eyes. It hurt me too, but I'm tired of trying to make it out to be more than it probably is.

"If you're here for a reason, then it's bigger than just your fucking living arrangements. It lies within the club, and secrets could blow us apart."

I don't want to argue with him, but I'm not going to sit here and talk about this either.

"Look, feel free to dig into whatever may or may not be happening here while I get on with my life. If that's all you came to say, then you should leave."

I push the chair back and stand abruptly, folding my arms

across my chest and nodding my head silently, telling them to leave.

Neither of them move a muscle to leave. I hate that I get so angry when Cas is around. Sparky could stay here all day and I wouldn't mind, but with Sparky comes Cas.

Choosing to ignore them both, I walk over and pick up the brush I'd been using and dip it into the paint. If they want to stay and be ignored, so be it.

When I hear movement behind me, I think they're finally leaving. Instead, Sparky bends down on his knees beside me and takes the brush away from me.

I look at him sharply, his face wore a different expression. I didn't think telling him to leave would hurt him this much.

"I need to tell you something else too," he says quietly.

"What?"

His brows knit together and he frowns. Throwing one quick look at Cas, he looks back to me and takes a deep breath.

"Micky was found dead yesterday. He was tortured and left at the state line."

No, he couldn't be dead. To me, he is—was, invincible. One of the original members. Before he lost his wife Flo to cancer, he, like Oak, was a big part of my life. He was the one who worked on his bike and didn't mind answering any questions I had—and believe me, I had many. He answered them all with the patience of a saint. Before he went nomad, he taught me to aim and shoot a gun. He said I couldn't always rely on someone else to defend me, and I had to learn for myself.

The tears don't come immediately. I suppose it's the shock.

When Sparky doesn't say anything further, that this isn't a joke, that's when I begin gasping for breath. The tears quickly follow, and I'm being crushed in his arms. He does his best to soothe me, and I let him. He'd done some bad things in his life that I had heard about, but he didn't deserve this. I cry harder, unable to control the pain invading me.

"All I've been doing is moaning about being here while he was out there somewhere, being..."

"Shhh," he coos.

"I have to call Aunt Kitty. She's going to need all the help she can get with the funeral," I say, feeling a little better with something to focus on.

A biker funeral is nothing to underestimate. Members from all over will attend, and they eat more than the population of a small country.

"No, you don't. He may not be having a funeral," he replies, almost reluctantly.

"The hell he isn't!" I shout. "What the fuck is wrong with you? He was your brother."

I roughly wipe my eyes dry with my paint encrusted sleeve and glare at him.

"He may have turned rat, Barbs. You know how that ends."

Oh, I know how it ends. He'll end up in an unmarked grave somewhere with no respect to his body or his soul.

No. I don't believe he would do this.

"He would never go against the club, and fuck you for thinking he did," I cry out, banging my fists against his chest.

"I don't want to believe it any more than you do, but it ain't looking good."

"I don't believe it, and I never will," I whisper.

Still in his Sparky's arms, I look to Cas, his expression telling me nothing of what he thinks regarding Micky. When I see pity for me in his eyes, I close mine to keep from seeing it.

"What's going on, Sparks? This is all getting out of control."

"I know. We're going to figure this shit out, and then we'll fucking cry, okay?"

I nod in agreement and pull away from him, wiping my eyes once again.

His phone begins ringing, and he stands up to answer it. After about thirty seconds, he hangs up and hugs me one more time, his promises to me muffled as he kisses the top of my head.

He says goodbye to Cas and leaves, alone. It brings it home that he could end up like Micky, walking out and never returning. I definitely couldn't deal with that.

Tears start to burn my eyes again, and I hold onto the kitchen cabinet for support. Cas is immediately at my side, taking hold of me. I could easily let him support me the same as Sparky did, but I'm not interested in his on and off attention.

Pushing away from him, I go to retrieve the paint brush and begin painting, hoping he'll take the hint and leave.

No such luck. He comes over and leans against the back door, a mere few feet away from me. The quick look I give him tells me it's useless to argue. He's not going anywhere.

I don't know how long we sit there, but I know I've painted the same section of wall three times.

"My aunt was sick once when I had a spelling bee. When Micky heard she wouldn't be able to go, he was the first one to turn up and sit center row. His cheers when I got the spelling of a word correct boomed through the auditorium." I laugh half-heartedly, remembering that day.

"Did you win?" he asked, his voice cracking from being silent for so long.

"No. I got stuck on one word. One of the teachers saw Micky mouthing the spelling to me and disqualified me." I sigh loudly before asking him, "Do you think he died a rat?"

I see confusion pass over his face before he speaks, so his answer doesn't surprise me.

"I honestly don't know. It's not what I want to believe, but like Sparky said, it ain't looking good, babe."

He sits forward, closer to me. "I know this isn't the time, but I need you to know, what you saw last night wasn't what you think it was. Nothing happened, and it wasn't going to either."

There it is again, the sincerity in his voice. It's even in his expression. I want him. I want him so bad I ache, but the last time I started to believe him, he ended up with a whore on his lap and his hands everywhere on her.

I force myself to look away from him and continue to paint the already covered patch on the wall.

"It's your business who and what you do. Just like it's my business who and what I do." He surprises me when he begins laughing. It's not just a chuckle, but a full-on laugh.

"Glad I amuse you," I mutter, not quite understanding why he finds it so funny.

"Oh, you amuse me all right. If you think anyone is coming near you, apart from me, then you're crazy, woman. I thought I made myself clear on that the other night."

His smile isn't cocky. It's the same smile I only saw last summer when he was with me.

Fuck, fuck, fuck! I can't deal with his smooth talking right now, but the small smile spreading across my lips, and the way I'm fidgeting, trying to hide my need for him, gives me away. He knows I'm close to giving in, but luckily, his ringtone sounds in his pocket, alerting him to club business. He'll have to go, and I'll be out of his charming-my-panties-off reach.

He pulls me up with him and holds me close. I know he more than likes me, so I don't know why he acts the way he does when I'm not around.

I should push him away. With what he did to me, I shouldn't hope he'll kiss me, but he does, and I let him.

It doesn't last nearly as long as I would've liked.

"I have to go," is all he says as he turns to leave.

I follow him and call out before he gets to the door,

"I don't like playing games, and I'm not into sharing."

He turns around and walks back to me.

"Neither do I, but at the moment, it feels like we're in one big fucking game. I have to play and prove to you I'm serious. I need to win."

Why does he have to say things like that? The usual butterflies in the stomach and going weak in the knees commences, and I want to hear more.

"What you did to me..."

"I know what I did to you. One day, you'll see the game started a long time ago. I need you to forgive me because I need you. And so you know, I don't want to be shared. Not when it comes to you," he says matter-of-factly.

This kiss between us lasts longer than the last. I don't have a clue if he's playing me this time or not, but he's making it harder for me to disbelieve him.

"One day soon, I'll tell you everything, and hopefully you'll trust me again."

Before I can say a word, he's throwing his leg over his bike and starting the engine. With one last look over his shoulder, he takes off and is gone, the sound of his bike disappearing through the trees.

## Cas

We've been over the details so many times, we're going around in circles.

"Has it occurred to anyone we could be walking into a trap tomorrow?" Slade asserts to the members at the table.

It would be pretty fucking stupid of us not to think it's a trap. Carving the word *RAT* on a man's forehead kind of implies they know our business and are going to show their faces one way or another.

"Of course I have!" Michael bellows. "But what choice do we have? Every time we try to take them out, we fuckin' fail."

I remain silent, listening to them hash it out. Slade has a point, and we can't dismiss it. Michael also has a point, and we can't dismiss that either.

I run my hands through my hair in frustration.

"They're expecting us to think they're going to show up. They're going to be prepared, but so will we. The drop-off warehouse is off the grid. If it comes to a fight, then we'll be ready. I'm tired of this shit happening. We fight, and we end this," I growl, not fucking around any longer.

"If we leave earlier than planned, we could plot up on higher ground somewhere and wait for them rather than ride into their trap," I add.

I look around the table at everyone nodding their agreement.

"So, we're all agreed. We'll go on the run tomorrow with nothing but empty fuckin' packages, and wait to see what happens?" Michael questions, finalising the details from this long ass meeting.

Nodding heads and murmurs of yesses go around the table, and Michael bangs the gavel hard. Meeting over.

I don't stick around long, leaving before Michael can put the gavel down. As the meeting went on, I felt more and more restless. Nothing about this feels right to me. The possibility of it being a set up by the Raging Riders being raised is no doubt true. If they're planning something against us, and we're going to attack tomorrow, we'll be ready for them.

The thought of staying at the clubhouse fills me with apprehension. I want to be back at the cabin, but I have a long way to go to gain Alannah's trust. The last couple of times I've been with her, I broke her down. I'm under no illusion that she hated herself after I left, though, and that's what I intend to change.

I pull up at the cabin to the prospect holding his gun on the porch. He relaxes when he recognises me, and again I question his presence here. I'm frustrated at not knowing the answer.

"Finished decorating?" I ask him.

Alannah seems to have taken to him for some reason. I don't remember her being friendly with a prospect before she went to college. She knew how it worked. Maybe it's being forced here with him? I trust her judgement, so if she's taken to him, he must okay.

"Yeah. She's cleaning, putting everything back in its place."

"Good. You can take off for the night. I'll stay and keep an eye on things," I tell him, lighting up a cigarette.

His eye begins twitching. Everyone is going to know his tell, because that twitch proves that he's either hiding something or nervous about someone.

"Michael said I shouldn't leave her."

"Michael isn't here. I'm your VP, prospect, and I say you can go for the fucking night."

He doesn't want to leave, but he begrudgingly does as he's told and walks to his truck.

"Be back by sunrise," I yell out.

He stopped and turned around, looking embarrassed.

"Um, what time's sunrise?"

I can't help but laugh.

"Figure it out."

~

Flicking the cigarette onto the gravel, I blow out the smoke and open the door. The house is silent, apart from the occasional clatter coming from the only room with a light on —the kitchen.

She watches me enter the room and continues to clean up.

I shrug out of my cut and jacket and hang them on the back of the chair, where I take a seat.

I'm content to sit and wait until she's ready to talk. I don't care how long it takes for her to forgive me. I'll go at her speed.

I watch as she finishes the cleaning and begins pulling packets out of the fridge.

She finally stops and gives me her attention.

"Are you staying long enough to eat?" she inquires.

Definitely progress, as there's no sarcasm in her voice.

I nod and remain silent. Her eyes are red and puffy, but they're dry. I hope for her sake, Micky, the man she knew and loved, hasn't betrayed us.

She whips up a quick meal, looking comfortable in knowing her way around the kitchen. Before long, she serves us both up some sort of a stir fry, which smells great. I rarely get to eat a proper home-cooked meal. I'm not even surprised at how good the food is. To me, this girl can do no fucking wrong.

She wants to speak, but something's stopping her, so I take it upon myself to start. It might not be what she wants to talk about, but I can't stop myself. I need to know.

"Do you think you'll be able to forgive me?" I brace myself for her reply.

"When I'm with you, and you're telling me you want me and don't want to be shared, I want to," she admits, albeit hesitantly as she pushes her food around her plate. "When you leave, I don't know what or who you're doing. I don't want to turn into a jealous, paranoid, crazy bitch, just to spend scraps of time with you whenever you want me."

"I don't want that for you either. What I did to you, I was forced into, and I complied for purely selfish reasons on my part." I can see the confusion etched on her face, so I continue. "I don't want anything or anyone to hurt you, especially me. What I felt for you last summer was real, Lana. I tried to stay away from you when you came back, but I don't want to. I want what we had before if you can give me that. And I'll give you all of me, I swear to you. You're all I need and want, no one else," I plead, hoping she believes me.

"I want you too," she says quietly.

I can see she wants me, but the pain I caused her is still there.

"That's good…that's progress," I reason, making her laugh.

"Yeah, progress. You throw me a few lines and I forgive it all," she snorts.

"Lana, don't do that. I don't think for one fucking second you've forgiven me for anything, but I'll prove it to you somehow, just how much you mean to me."

For the past year, her face is all I've seen. No amount of booze and pussy took that away.

I can still see the doubt deep in her eyes, but she accepts my declaration and raises her chin as she asks, "Are you staying tonight?"

"I would like to," I reply, taking hold of her hand.

Deciding not to push her any further, I remember the stash upstairs we keep here for backup.

"Come with me," I say, pulling her out of her chair.

Taking her upstairs, she probably thinks I'm taking her to bed, which I'm tempted to do. Instead, I open the door to an oversized cupboard.

"I forgot this was here," she gasps, looking around at the assortment of weapons.

"You knew about this?" Quite frankly, I'm surprised.

"Of course. I did grow up in the club, you know. I used to stay here sometimes with my dad," she says with a smile. "Obviously, I was warned to death not to touch them. It used to have a big lock on the door."

Of course she knew about them. Sometimes I forget she's been a part of the club since birth, only being hidden from serious club business.

"Do I need to ask if you know how to use one?"

She doesn't reply. Instead, takes hold of a Glock and loads it with the ammunition next to it. Within seconds, the gun is ready for use.

"I'll take that as a yes," I laugh as she giggles, unloading her handiwork.

"That's pretty hot you know how to do that," I smirk as she puts the gun back in its place.

For the rest of the night, we settle on the sofa, watching a movie neither of us are interested in, but happy enough just to be together. This is the first time I've given my attention to any woman in this way, just long enough to fuck them and be on my way. But now, sitting on a sofa that has seen better days with Alannah snuggled against me, I find myself never wanting this moment to end. Tomorrow's run fills me with nothing but stress. Having her in my arms makes anything seem possible, that everything will work out. It has to now. All I have to do is prove to her I mean what I say, and I'll be able to call her mine, then sort out how I'm going to tell Michael.

After a while, she falls asleep, snuggled up against me. I carefully pick her up and take her up the stairs to bed.

My cock begs me to wake her up, slide in beside her, and take her from all sides. Literally having to tell my cock to shut the fuck up, I strip to my boxers and pull the covers back to join her. She isn't like the club whores, and I'm not intending to treat her like one. It's not hard to see how much I get to her, but I need her to want me like she did last year. The closest I get to her is pulling her back against my chest. She murmurs something incoherently, and holds onto my arm across her stomach. Oh God, this is where I need to be, with her like this every god damn night.

Sleep doesn't come easy. If I'm not thinking about the next day's upcoming event, Alannah is moving against me, and setting my cock off again and again.

Finally succumbing to sleep, I hear the prospect's truck pull up. Surely it can't be that time already?

Groaning quietly as to not wake her, I gently roll her to the side and rise from the bed. Quietly dressing, I keep my eyes on her the whole time. She truly is beautiful.

Bending over the bed, I place a soft kiss on her lips.

"I think... I think I love you," I whisper, barely loud enough for even myself to hear.

# 5

## Cas

We ride to the warehouse as we usually do on any normal run. Everything looks the same, nothing around us seeming out of place. We ride close to each other, keeping our formation tight in case of an ambush, and stop in front of the warehouse doors. Normally we make the drop-off and our brothers from the Devil's Bastards take over and deliver the packaged drugs to where they need to go. Lincoln, their President, has been told of the changes, and will take over as usual at the end of the week.

Inside, the warehouse is empty, but for few tables and chairs here and there, and nothing else. Pope and Slade bring in the fake, empty packages and throw them on the table. We'd normally wait around for a while, have a smoke, stretch our legs and leave. So today, we do exactly that. If any Raging fuck is around watching us, we won't look suspicious.

Keeping our cool is difficult, as everyone is tense. Their hands continually twitch on their guns, ready to pull out if anyone turns up.

I take a seat on one of the chairs, carefully testing it to make sure it can hold my weight. Pope takes the position at the door, keeping a lookout. The road in is straight, so we'll have plenty of warning if they come cruising in now.

"There's a slip off about a mile up the main road. We take that, then we can get a good view if they turn up," Slade informs us, tapping on his phone.

Michael looks at his watch, and then looks at us.

"We'll give it ten minutes, then we go."

~

So far, the drop-off has gone off without a hitch, not one peep of a Raging Rider in sight. Mostly sitting in silence on our bikes, everyone is beginning to feel the strain of the cold setting in.

"How much longer are we going to wait, boss?" Sparky asks, blowing into his hands to keep them warm.

Michael's been getting more and more impatient as time passes. I don't know what he expected. It's not like the Raging Riders were going to turn up as we were leaving. Well, I wouldn't plan that myself, so I gathered they wouldn't either.

"Another hour, then we'll fuck off home," he answers, loud enough for everyone to hear.

Our chapter is relatively small in numbers, each of us bringing a certain flair to the club. It has only been in the last year Michael began taking in prospects again. Other chapters of the club have up to forty members each, with ours only holding sixteen.

After the drop-off at the old, battered warehouse, we backtracked and set up watch on higher ground where Slade had told us. We could see everything. Just as the hour is nearly up, just before three in the morning, we see headlights driving up the secluded road.

"Here we go, boys," Slade announces, with a touch of excitement.

It's been so boring, I feel my heart start to race, feeling the buzz of excitement soar through the men. I don't think it's sunk in yet that seeing our rivals here means that Micky had, in fact, turned *rat*. But I'll keep my mouth shut until we're clear of this situation.

We keep watch on the van, and as it comes closer, we all feel positive it's the Raging Riders.

They stop by the warehouse, and three men get out, warily looking around the place.

"Prospects," Sparky hisses.

Michael begins cursing. This isn't what we were hoping for. What are we going to gain from the fucking prospects? No doubt they've been sent to scope out the area. There was no fight to be had tonight.

They quickly exit the building, and one of them is tapping on his phone.

"Fuck this," Michael snaps.

Before I can get to him, he has his gun in hand, and is aiming at the three men.

They're not who we're after. It's an unnecessary attack.

He pulls the trigger, and the one with the phone goes down, shot in the leg.

The rest of us pull our weapons out, ready in case of retaliation. The other two are looking around frantically, helping the wounded man into the back of the van. It's apparent they're not armed. By the time I finish telling the others to fall back, the three prospects are in the van and speeding away.

"That wasn't your fuckin' call!" Michael bellows.

"You weren't going to fucking call it. The pussies weren't even armed."

"Shit... Fuck...This has been one hell of a wasted fuckin' night!" he yells, kicking at the dirt beneath his boots in frustration.

"It's been a night of revelations."

Everyone looks at Pope. He doesn't speak often, but when he does, everyone listens. I already know what he's referring to.

"Proves Micky fucked us over."

Having said that, he sits on his bike, kickstarts it and rides off. None of us wanted to believe it was true, but tonight's events clarified it is.

"Back to square one. We'll drive back and get some sleep. Then tonight, we'll figure this shit out."

The air is thick with tension as Micky's betrayal and the flop that happened tonight sinks in.

No one says a word as we prepare for the ride back. We won't make it back to Willow's Peak until the afternoon, and by then, no one will say anything and go straight to bed.

Too much is up in the air in my life, and I'm not liking it. When I first came to the club, life wasn't this wild. We had run-ins with other clubs while on runs of our own, but that was our life and we took it on. Shit, these days are much more intense than back then. They seem like a walk in the fucking park compared to now. Each attack on the club, every decision Michael is making, feels wrong. The only thing that feels right is getting close to Alannah. If I knew a year ago what life would be like now, I would've gone against Michael and called his bluff at tossing me out of the club and kept Alannah with me. I would've found a job somewhere close to her college and began a new life with her. The family I chose over her wasn't the same as it is today. The club is changing, and I don't think I'll last much longer being a part of it unless the changes are for the better.

~

The ride home holds none of the joy it normally does. Riding behind Michael, we're the first ones to see the bullet holes covering the entire gate that encloses the clubhouse. Windows are shot through, and none of the prospects are anywhere to be seen.

Slade comes up behind us, gets off his bike, and punches in the code to open the gates. As we ride in, the garage door and shutters are all closed, the clubhouse barricaded up, and no one's in sight.

No wonder the Raging Riders sent prospects. They were planning an attack here the whole time.

"Everyone, check the clubhouse. I'm going to check on Kitty," Michael growls, running toward his house.

Getting over the shock, my mind opens to the possibility that Alannah could be in danger too. Quickly retrieving my phone from my side bag, I tear my glove off with my teeth and scroll down the list for the prospect's number.

It rings and rings. No answer. I try three more times before I lose my temper and leave him a message, demanding he answer his fucking phone.

Shoving the phone back in the side bag and yanking on my glove, I roar my bike back to life and ride out of the compound.

Cursing all the way to the cabin for being too far from the clubhouse, I eventually make it there in one piece, shocking myself at how I didn't run myself off the road with the speed I was going at.

The prospect's truck is still parked in the same place as when I left a couple of days ago. Nothing seems out of place, no sense of danger. Nothing.

I take my gloves and helmet off, and then pull the bandana down around my neck. I'm about to call Sparky to see what's going on back at the clubhouse when I hear a gunshot, causing my heart to slam to the ground. Recovering quickly, I pull my gun out of the side bag and make off around the side of the cabin where I heard the shot come from.

Alannah

The last couple of days, I've been on a confused high. Cas wants me, and not only that, he wants—no, he *needs* me to forgive him. I was truthful when I told him I wanted to, but there's still a small part of me that doesn't understand why he did what he did to me. He said he was a playing a game, although not with me. It started a long time ago. Maybe it has something to do with that? If it was, then it's a cruel game I definitely don't want to play.

Sitting at the table in the freshly decorated kitchen, I look around and find it makes the rest of the house look dim and dingy. Billy still hasn't left. He stayed, regardless of me telling him I'd be fine on my own.

His insistence of staying this long is beginning to make me feel like there's something my uncle is hiding from me. I've sat all morning, mug after mug of coffee, pondering scenario after scenario of what could be going on, coming to no concrete conclusion. Most often, each scenario would always end with me in danger, or why else have me protected?

Deciding to give up on thinking, I wash the mug and put it to dry on the drainer. Making my way to the cupboard that has always been off limits to me, I open the door to find what I need.

Putting them in a duffle bag, I go back downstairs to find Billy. Since the kitchen is finished, he spends most of his time on the front porch. Opening and closing the door behind me, I nudge my foot against his and his eyes shoot open.

"Come on, I've had an idea," I tell him as I head down to the stairs. I turn around to see if he's following, but he's already right behind me.

"This is going to be so much fun," I beam.

After forty minutes of target practice at the back of the cabin, we have one bullet each left.

"Your turn," I giggle.

"I think I should be getting lessons from you," he remarks.

With each shot he takes, he gets more wound up. My aim is sharper than his, and he doesn't like it.

He takes his last shot and it goes wide. I can tell he's trying to rein in his anger for my sake, which makes me laugh quietly.

I hold my position and take aim of the bottle sitting on the cutoff tree trunk. I admit, I'm just showing off now.

As I squeeze the trigger, my name being yelled from behind makes me jump, and as a result, my shot goes wide as well. I turn toward the voice and see Cas running around the cabin, holding his gun and searching all around us. Seeing the alarm, Billy quickly pulls his gun from behind his back and begins doing the same.

Cas doesn't stop running until he has me in his arms. I thought he was angry by the way he was yelling my name. However, from the way he's holding me, I quickly decipher he's in fact, anxious. I pull back from him and see pure terror radiating from him. I can't look away, and neither can he. Billy mumbles something before walking off, leaving us alone. All I can think of is that whatever has happened, he came to me.

"Hey, what's going on?"

"What are you doing out here?" he asks, without answering my question first.

"I was bored, so I thought I'd get some shooting practice in."

"Thank fuck," he mutters, searching my eyes intently.

I take hold of his hand and lead him back into the cabin, and he doesn't hesitate to follow.

Once inside, I can hear my own heartbeat in the calmness of the house. I lead him through to the lounge and sit on the sofa where he joins me, and this time he grasps my hand tight in his. This is a defining moment in how our relationship is going to continue, and I plan to make the most of it because I want him with every ounce of my being.

"I want to be with you. I want to forget everything that's happened, and I want everything we had last time." I surprise myself with how strong I sound, and that's good. I want him to know I'm not to ever be treated like that again.

A stray tear falls down my cheek when he kisses my hand repeatedly before looking up at me.

"That's all I want too. I can't tell you enough how sorry I am, but Lana, you're the best thing that's ever happened to me, and I'm not going to risk losing you again."

"I need you to understand, I won't be like the other women, hanging onto her man no matter what he does behind her back so she doesn't lose him," I warn him, meaning every word. "If you want to be with me, then there'll be no one else," I add.

"I promise, you're all I want. I haven't fucked anyone since you've been back," he vows.

"I think it's time you told me what happened last year." I don't really want to hear all the details, but deep down, I know I have to so we can move forward.

His expression soon changes from relief to agitation, and he grasps my hand tighter, as if he's worried I'll slip through his fingers.

He inhales deeply.

"Remember the last day we spent together?" I can't help but roll my eyes and nod. Did he seriously think I'd forget?

"You had gone home, and I went to find Michael. I wanted to ask his permission to be with you. Spending time together like we did was going against your uncle's rules, and I didn't want to keep going behind his back. I thought if I could explain to him how I felt about you, and he could see how genuine my feelings for you were, he would give us his blessing. I was on top of the fucking world walking toward the garages where he was, only he wasn't alone. Every brother was there waiting for me, all lined around in a semicircle. I knew immediately he already knew."

My stomach lurches into my throat. Usually, if all the brothers were in the garages with no big job to work on, it meant violence.

"Go on," I urge.

"Michael made a big speech about how a brother had disrespected another brother in the club, a brother who happens to be our President. He'd found out about us and asked if I'd deny it. I didn't, since there was no point in lying. I told him I knew it was wrong, but I couldn't help having feelings for you."

He pauses, seeming as if he doesn't want to continue, but he straightens his shoulders and goes on with the story.

"In the end, I took a couple of hits from each brother. Michael went last and drove his point home that you and me were never going to happen. After they finished with me, I was a crumpled mess on the floor, but I pulled myself up and told him I couldn't give you up, that they could beat me every day if it meant I got to be with you."

I'm right to feel sick. I've seen this punishment handed out before. It doesn't sound so bad taking a couple of hits from a few members, but when there's fifteen or so men giving their best shot to your face and ribs, the results are the same as getting beaten to a pulp.

"Half the guys respected I was being genuine after forcing myself to stand and look Michael in the eye. I expected him to hit me again, but he spoke. He asked me if I loved you. At the time, you'd messed my head up so much I couldn't think straight. I liked being with you, but I didn't know what love was, or if I felt that for you. So, I told him no, and he warned me that if he caught me with you again, he would strip my VP patch and throw my ass out of the club."

Fuck. How do I respond to that? I don't have to, because he apparently has more to say.

"Like I said, I knew I liked you more than anyone else, but to lose the one aspect of my life that felt right shook the fuck out of me. To lose it over a girl I didn't truly know how I felt about was worse. The guys started to leave, and Michael told me to fix it before you left for college. He didn't want you gaining further ideas about us."

This time, I can't stop myself. I know exactly what I want to ask.

"So, how does that whore fit into this?"

"With you knowing the ways of the club, I knew I would have to do something drastic for you to believe I didn't want to see you again, that nothing more could happen between us, and if you saw the bruises I'd received, you wouldn't have let it go."

He inhales so deeply, I think he was going to release his breath.

"Thinking like a prick, I grabbed the first girl I saw in the clubhouse when I got back and took her to my room. Just her presence in there made me sick because I wanted it to be you like we'd planned. Just before you were due…well, you know what I did."

Once again, I'm speechless. His betrayal wasn't what I thought it was. It was because of my uncle, though Cas chose how to act. After I left for college, it hurt bad. That night was continually on replay in my mind, but I couldn't understand why after how close we had become that summer. At the time, I knew it didn't make sense, but I guess it does now.

"So, you didn't do it on purpose?" No, he can't justify it. I know this. But I want to make sure I understand.

"There was a purpose, Lana, and it's haunted me ever since," he admits.

It still hurts remembering that night, but at least I know the reason. Will I forget the scene I saw or how it made me feel? Hell no. But knowing my uncle beat and threatened him with his place in the club over something that was really none of his business, it didn't hurt as much.

"What's changed from then to now?" I inquire.

If he slept with that whore to keep me away from him and his patch, then why risk it now?

"Everything's changing. The club is becoming something I don't recognise, and not in a good way. I feel you have something to do with that. Last year, I thought the club was all I lived for, but since you've been back, I want to live for you."

Wow, he certainly knows what to say to make me weak. Not only in the knees, but all over.

"Does you knowing this change anything?" he asks, looking sheepish as he waits for my reply.

I don't need to think about it. Although, I have a few stipulations for him if this is going to work.

"No."

He visibly relaxes and goes to pull me onto his lap until I stop him.

"But, I know to share you with the club. And by club, I mean club business and the brothers, not the whores throwing themselves at you. If you truly mean what you say, then I should be more than enough for you."

"You are," he insists, and I finally let him guide me onto his lap and wrap my arms around his neck.

He thinks he's home free and begins kissing along my jawline. However, I'm not finished.

"Just so we're clear, you're not my Vice President. To me, you're just Cas, and if you betray me again, I will kill you."

He grips my chin and forces me to look at him.

"I don't need a fucking incentive not to hurt you again. Trust me."

"I will. I'm just letting you know the consequences," I smirk, leaning in to claim his lips as he leans forward.

The bedroom isn't close enough. I begin ripping my top off as he starts unhooking my bra. Taking my nipple into his mouth, he bites down and sucks it hard before moving across to my other nipple to do the exact same thing to it. He kneads my breasts roughly, causing me to whimper with the pressure he's exerting. My need to feel him inside me matches his need to feel me. We practically tackle each other, both of us trying to get the other's jeans off as we fall on top of each other and onto the floor.

It starts as a serious longing to be as close as possible, but crashing to the floor like a movie cliché, I can't help but giggle.

"That sound makes me harder."

His animalistic growl and warm breath against my neck sobers me up. He's so fucking hot.

Rolling me to my side, he lays down behind me, pushing himself against me. I arch my back, grinding my ass into his groin when he thrusts inside of me, moving slowly, in and out, in and out. Squeezing down on my breast, the force of his thrusts change from slow and sensual to hard and fast, causing me to spiral out of control. The more he carries on like this, the less I can think. But what I do know is, my mind is on a single mission, and that's to lose myself to this man.

Craning my head back, I kiss him feverishly as he moves inside of me. I don't have to tell him what I like or how I like it, he just knows, and he's taking great pleasure in doing so.

Just as I'm considering changing position, wanting him on top of me so I can look at him, he glides his hand down and rubs my clit, adding the right amount of pleasure, never ceasing his tirade of internal torment. He's not going to last much longer, his hips moving more erratically, but he wants me to finish too. His hands working their magic everywhere tips me over the edge and into fucking bliss.

Once we'd come down and our breathing had evened out, we lied there in each other's arms as he explained how the clubhouse had been attacked while they were on their run, and when he heard Billy and I practicing out back, how he assumed the worst.

"Until this is under control, I don't want you leaving this cabin. I'd fight for you any day, but I'd rather you not to be in danger in the first place," he insists, stroking my hair as I lay on his chest.

"I don't have anywhere to go at the moment, so that works for me," I assure him.

"That was easier than I thought it would be."

"What are we going to do about us?" I question, choosing to ignore his dig.

I don't want him losing his place in the club for me. I also don't want him to have to choose.

"I don't know, baby, but I'll think of something."

My post orgasm high begins dwindling away, giving me room to think about my plans for redecorating.

I move off him and lean on my elbow so he can see my face.

"I have to leave the cabin one more time, actually. I want to redecorate in here too, and for that I need to go to the hardware store again."

If I'm going to be on a secret cabin lockdown, then I damn well want something to occupy my time while Cas isn't here.

"Write a list and I'll get one of the other prospects to go

shopping. I'm serious, Lana. I don't want anything to happen to you because you want to fucking paint."

"Okay. I'll get Billy on it before you go," I relent, settling back on his chest.

"Who the fuck is Billy?" he snaps, none too happy.

"Surely the Vice President knows the names of his prospects?" I tease, feeling his heartbeat slowly return to normal.

"Oh. I didn't, actually," he laughs. "Okay, I should get back. I kind of left not knowing what actually happened or if anyone was hurt."

It's completely selfish, but I'm glad he came straight to me.

"Okay."

We both get up from the floor and salvage our clothes from all corners of the room, neither of us taking our eyes of each other as we do.

When he finds his phone, he looks down at the screen and curses.

"Get the prospect on that list. I really need to go."

"His name is Billy," I call out, leaving to go find him.

Within five minutes, Billy has asked me the colours I want, and has added any extra equipment we would need and hands the list over to Cas. I listen to Cas tell him that we're not to go anywhere, and that my uncle doesn't need to know these new arrangements, or the fact that he'll be around more often.

After he finishes giving him his new orders, Billy leaves us alone on the front porch.

It feels reassuring knowing he really does need to leave

yet takes the time to say goodbye to me without it feeling rushed.

"I'll be back as soon as I can," he promises.

"You better be," I order him with a smile.

"We're going to have to keep this between us for the time being." I nod my understanding.

"Then, when all the Raging Rider shit is sorted, I'm going to tell everyone you're my old lady, and anyone who has a problem with us can go fuck themselves," he grins menacingly.

"Sounds good to me."

We share one last kiss on the porch and he leaves on his bike, where I stand long after he leaves. There's no way my uncle is going to run my life anymore. Hell, he's already pushed me out of the club and into seclusion. I'm not going to lose Cas because of him.

I don't doubt my uncle loves me. He's only wanted the best for me since he took me on as a grief-stricken six-year-old, but to say who I can and can't fall in love with is going too far.

One afternoon was all it took for my life to completely change and going back would only destroy me.

# 6

## Cas

Sparky's waiting for my return as I ride toward the compound. He closes the gate behind me as I ride through and park my bike in the garage.

"Michael's pissed with you for disappearing," he informs me as soon as I cut the engine.

"I don't give a fuck. I'm back now."

"I take it you've been with Barbie?"

"Yeah, and I need to talk to you once I've seen Michael."

"Sure. She all right?" he asks as we stroll into the clubhouse and through to the back room where church is held.

"She's more than good," I grin. He doesn't have time to ask what I mean as we arrive, finding everyone already seated.

"Nice of you to fuckin' join us, Cas," Michael sneers from the other end of the table.

"I'm here now," I point out as we take our seats. "Do we know what happened?"

"One of the prospects on lookout saw Raging Riders ride past, pull out guns and open fire..." As Oak is explaining, the table erupts into chaos.

"I say we do a drive-by of our own," Slade announces, smirking at the possibility.

"Yeah, take them all out."

This is no good. My brothers are out for blood and revenge, and not thinking properly. We would probably have the same amount of luck they did—too many bullets wasted and no lives lost.

No, what we need is a better, well-thought-out plan that wouldn't impact the club, but bring down the Raging Riders once and for all.

I call for quiet and wait for everyone to calm down enough to listen. Once I have everyone's attention, I speak quietly and precisely so they understand what I'm saying. I don't want to repeat myself.

"Let's face it, they'll be waiting for a retaliation, and lives could be lost on our side too. Instead of exposing ourselves like that, what if we could take them out without wasting a single bullet?"

I have their attention now.

"What are you thinking, Cas?" Michael inquires, leaning forward on the table.

"I'm thinking we use Sparky's expertise and take them out in one fell swoop. They don't allow any women in their compound, so we don't need to worry about innocents."

Sparky's expertise is playing with explosives.

"Fuck yeah. I haven't been able to play in ages. What a comeback that would be." Sparky bangs his fists numerous times on the tabletop in excitement.

I look to Michael to see what he thinks about it, his mouth pulling up at the corner tells me he likes it.

"This is why you're my VP, you brainy shit." A full-blown grin spreads across his face.

"Everyone agree?"

No one's against it. They're not getting the blood the way they wanted to, but none of them can refuse a blowout.

"Slade get whatever Sparky needs to make this happen," he orders, before adding, "You have one week. We'll hit them next Saturday."

"We should go on lockdown until we take them out," Oak interjects, which is a pretty good idea. If we're on lockdown, then Alannah would be here, close to me, and safe.

"No!" Michael snaps. He doesn't even give any thought to it, just a straight-out refusal.

"Look what happened while we weren't around? Imagine what they could do if we *are* around? No one's safe until they're dealt with," Oak argues.

"There's no need for lockdown yet. We'll keep our eyes open, and if, and I mean *if*, anything happens over the next few days, we'll reevaluate."

"Michael, our loved ones were shot at today, and you want to leave them unprotected? You can't fuckin' expect the prospects to be enough to keep them safe when we're gone next week."

Everyone can see Michael is losing his patience, but Oak

doesn't care. He's known Michael long enough to know how far he can push him.

"Fine. Keep your families close, and when we leave on Saturday, all old ladies and the girls can go and stay with Alannah at the cabin. It's off the radar, and all prospects will go with them," he compromises.

Oak knows that's the best he's going to get out of Michael, so he nods his agreement and leaves the room.

"Thank God none of us has any children, or there wouldn't be any fuckin' room," Michael tries to joke. It's no good. No one's in a good mood, and a simple joke isn't going to help.

Everyone leaves the room and goes their own way. I pull Sparky toward the bar and get us each a beer.

"So, you and Alannah, huh?"

"Yeah. We got a problem?"

"It was bound to happen. I hope you know what you're doing."

"I do. As soon as this bullshit is finished, I'll talk to Michael. But until then, you got my back?"

Normally, I wouldn't have to ask. In any situation he always has my back, but when it comes to Alannah, I have to make sure.

He narrows his eyes and keeps me waiting for his answer.

"I always have your back, brother. No changing it now. Just don't make me regret it by hurting her, 'cause I'd hate to put you down."

"As if you could," I laugh. "But I'm not going to hurt her again." And I'm serious.

Nodding, he looks behind me and straightens. Glancing

over my shoulder, I see Michael walking toward us. Something is definitely up with him, and I can't wait to find out what it is.

"Sparky, I need you to let Alannah know she's got company coming. Give her this. Tell her to make sure there's enough food, and to get more blankets," he advises, handing over a wad of cash.

He doesn't hang around. As soon as the cash is in Sparky's hand, he's gone again.

"As far as I know, he hasn't called Lana, and he hasn't asked about how she is. For someone who didn't want her living this life, he was pretty quick to use her for security. Doesn't that seem strange to you?" I ask, watching Michael retreat to his office.

"Maybe he asks the prospect on his daily updates?"

"Fuck knows. We leaving or what?"

"You coming with me?"

"Of course. I'm not going to miss a chance to see my old lady," I grin, careful to keep my voice low.

"I never thought I'd hear you say those words," he laughs, walking out in front of me.

Neither did I.

## Alannah

"How long have you been a prospect, Billy?" We're sitting at the table, eating a late dinner of spaghetti.

"About three months. Your uncle helped me out a couple of times, and I decided I wanted to join."

"How are you finding it?"

"It's okay. Been a lot better since I came here. I've never had so many home-cooked meals before." He smiles, almost sadly.

"What about your family? Are they from around here?"

"Nah. I'm on my own, always have been."

I've never gone without anything, so it always makes me feel sad when I hear some people didn't grow up with at least the necessities, such as food.

"Well, you're always welcome here for dinner, even after you're done babysitting me," I tell him, hoping he'll divulge a hint of information about his presence.

"Thanks, Alannah," he says before focusing on his food. I'm happy that he's dropped the "miss" before my name. It made me feel far too old for my actual age of twenty-two.

"I know you think I know why I'm here, but I honestly don't. I wouldn't lie to you now. I like you, Alannah."

Never in my life did I think I would make friends with a prospect, but like everything else that's happened in my life lately, there's always a first time for everything.

"And I meant, I like you as a friend, um... nothing more," he stutters, blushing furiously.

I can't help but burst out laughing.

"I know what you meant, Billy. I like you too, um... as a friend," I laugh harder when I mimic him.

After a couple of beats, he joins in too. I wasn't sure Billy would pass for a Lost Soul the first day I met him when he brought me here, but after spending time with him, I can see his loyalty, and when he's told to do something, he does it with everything he has.

We hear bikes approaching, and Billy is out of his chair, reaching for his gun. Disappearing down the hall, he opens the front door, and I hear him greet Sparky as he lets him inside.

Making his way back into the kitchen, Billy clears his plate and glass away before being told to leave by Sparky. When I turn around, I see he's not alone. Cas is with him. I have to force myself to keep from grinning, not wanting to give our secret away, and glare at Sparky.

"Stop telling him to leave every time you show up, *Jason*," I say sternly, because he hates it when I use his real name. "He's my friend, and if he wants to stay, he can."

"It's okay, Alannah. Really, it is," Billy says quietly as he leaves the room.

Dumping my plate in the sink, I take a seat at the table. Sparky has already taken his usual spot at the table by the door, while Cas follows Billy out.

"He'll be one of your brothers one day. You'll do well to remember that," I point out, just as Cas comes back.

I can't help the flutters in my stomach. Keeping our relationship a secret is going to be harder than I anticipated.

"And you'll do well to remember he's nothing but a fucking prospect. He'll earn our respect when he proves his loyalty to us. You know, all this isolation is fucking with your head, Barbie. I haven't forgotten the hell we used to put them through when we were younger," he smirks, reminding me of our hell-raising days.

"Yeah, well, he's the one I've been stuck here with for days now, so forgive me if I want to make friends," I reply bitterly.

"Well, we come with news you'll like, then."

"What?" I have a feeling I'm not going to like this.

"This Saturday, you'll have guests... about twenty of them."

What?

Who?

"We're all leaving on club business, and we need a place for all the old ladies to stay," Cas explains, speaking for the first time since he arrived.

I know better than to ask what they're going to be doing, but whatever they're planning, it must be serious for them to uproot the women and put them somewhere other than the clubhouse. No, I don't want to know—the less the better. Anyway, it'll be good to see everyone, especially Aunt Kitty.

"You cool with that?" Sparky snaps his fingers in my face, bringing me out of my musings.

"Of course. Just come home in one piece, please, both of you," I beg, remembering Micky's torturous demise.

"Always," he promises, knowing what I'm thinking.

I realize that I hadn't bothered to ask if they'd already eaten. Wanting to keep myself busy, I get up and make them each a plate of spaghetti. Serving their dinners in silence, I take a seat.

Sparky's so focused on shoveling food into his mouth, I take the opportunity to sneak a flirty grin at Cas. His wink and casual smirk has me feeling all warm and fuzzy inside, and wishing we were alone.

"This tastes good, Barbs. Cas has done well making you his old lady."

I snap my head toward Cas, who's grinning from ear to ear. After everything he said had gone down last year, and that we should keep it between ourselves, within a matter of hours he's gone and told someone. So much for secrecy.

"It's all right. I told him, and he's cool."

"So you didn't take part in hurting him last year?" I quip, knowing full well he did.

"You know the club. You knew what would happen to him when Michael found out about the two of you."

It's true, but it doesn't mean I agree with it.

"As long as you're happy, then so am I. Don't worry, I won't be saying nothing, and if events are to be repeated, I won't be taking part this time," he assures.

"Thank you."

I haven't had to keep secrets before—not that I've seen anyone to actually lie about our new relationship to—it doesn't really sit right with me. Sparky knowing about us takes the edge off the frustration I feel, and knowing one day we won't be a secret anymore makes it significantly different to last time.

"What are your plans for tonight?" I hope Cas is going to stay, and as much as I love Sparky, I hope he's planning to leave.

"I'm staying here with you tonight." Cas smiles, sliding my chair toward his and taking my hand. It's such a simple gesture, but for us, it's our first show of being a couple, even if it is only in front of one person.

"I have no plans, and in no rush to get back," Sparky replies.

I've been unhappy because I don't get many visitors, and here I am, silently begging Sparky to leave so I can have Cas to myself.

Then again, while he's here, he might as well put his muscles to good use and help me out with moving the furniture away from the walls in the lounge so it'll be ready to paint. If he leaves, not wanting to be domesticated, then I win too.

"What's with evil fucking grin?" he asks.

"You'll see."

After forty-five minutes of both Cas and Sparky complaining about doing the prospect's job, all the furniture has been shoved into the middle of the room to make room for us to paint. And by us, I mean mostly Billy.

"He's only one man, and I can't exactly help him with the heavier pieces, can I?"

"If having an old lady entails this kind of work, I'd rather stay on my own," Sparky groans, slumping into the plush, oversized armchair.

"And do you have anything to say?" I ask Cas, amused by how much they were bitching. I mean, for badass bikers, they sure are being overdramatic.

"Nope," he chirps, pulling me down with him onto the sofa.

Billy returns and hovers in the doorway.

"Where have you been?" I huff, sitting up a little straighter.

"Hardware store."

"It's not open this time of night."

"The owner is an old friend. I was quick, so he didn't mind staying open a little later than usual."

I'd learned so much about this prospect, but obviously, I didn't know everything.

"And you couldn't get me any discount?" I laugh. Not that I paid with my own cash last time.

"I did tonight. I'll bring it all in tomorrow morning."

Cas squeezes me tight against him and says to Billy, "Grab us some beers and come and join us."

I smile my gratitude and relax into the sofa. Billy's gone less than a minute and passes the beers around before making himself comfortable on the other armchair.

Nights like tonight are what I envisioned I'd have while I was away at college. I didn't foresee Cas being a part of this, but he is, and tonight couldn't be any more perfect. And the fact that Cas is making more of an effort with Billy shows me he really is trying for me.

"How did you get named Sparky?" Billy questions.

Both Cas and I laugh. Any opportunity for Sparky to talk about himself, he was in heaven.

"Well, things that go boom really get me going, know what I mean? Growing up, I had a certain flair for flares," he drawls. "I was at one school for a while before my dad moved us on again. He'd gotten it in his head I had to bring home no less than C's. I worked my fucking ass off for weeks on this science project—it was the tits—and when I handed it in, I got a D. I was pissed. I threw it across the class, and then smashed the lab up. Dad got pissed 'cause he got called into school, and I was suspended for a week. After we got home, I got a beating from my old man. I was fucking livid. I snuck out that night, taking one of my homemade plastic bottle creations and broke into the school."

"What did you do?" Billy prods, immersed in the story.

I roll my eyes. He's loyal, but he wasn't the sharpest knife in the drawer.

"What do you think I did? I blew up the fucking science department. Fucking teacher didn't know what he was talking about."

"No way," Billy barks out excitedly.

"Yes way. I left home not long after that, and that's when Michael found me, trying to blow one of his places up. Didn't know it was his, of course, but he stopped me and took me in. When I patched in, he gave me the name Sparky."

I close my eyes, listening to Sparky continue to tell Billy stories about the crap he's pulled over the years. It's not stuff you'd normally be proud of, but Billy's lapping it up. I'm content. I have my man by my side, my best friend's blessing, and a new life I'm creating.

# 7

## Alannah

I wake up expecting it to be dark outside, and still on the sofa with Cas. Instead it's morning, and I'm lying in bed with a very naked, and very sexy Cas. A girl's day couldn't begin any better. He must have carried me up sometime last night.

I manage to turn around without waking him up. His chest is free from the sheet, giving me the opportunity to study his tattoos more in-depth. Since last summer, there are more Lost Souls insignias on his biceps, as well as the full back piece all the brothers have. "Lost Souls" is tattooed across his collarbone in Old English script, with a date in roman numerals underneath—the date he became a full member. From top to bottom on the right side of his ribs, he has an intricate detailed sign of the cross, and on his left side, he has the same style cross, but it's tattooed on upside down.

Drawing my eyes away from his tattoos, I come back to his chest. I'd seen him working on his bike with his shirt off many times, and the sight always took my breath away. It's unbelievable how anyone can really have abs so defined. He looks like a walking photoshop advertisement.

Feeling the stirrings arising down below, I decide to wake him up. I run my finger softly across his abs, all the way down to where the sheet covers his bottom half. I've only moved the sheet an inch before I see him smile. He still has his eyes closed, but he knows what I'm up to, especially when I move the sheet, exposed him fully. My plan is to take him into my mouth and start his day with a bang, so to speak. He moves like lightning, and has me on my back before I can make my move.

"Good morning, baby," he says between kisses.

"Good morning yourself."

"I've been waiting for you to wake up," he growls against my neck, sending a shiver through my body.

"You should've woken me up last night."

"I was tempted to," he murmurs, snaking a path with his tongue between my breasts and down to my center. Taking my thighs in his large hands, he moves on to nip and kiss his way from my knee and back to where I want him the most. When he's finally there, his begins to devour me with his tongue. Every moan, every cry that leaves my lips, he drives his tongue deeper, harder. Digging my hands into the sheets, I gasp when I hear—

*Knock! Knock! Knock!*

Whoever's was on the other side of that door can fuck right off. This might as well be classed as the first time a man has gone down on me, because it never before felt this fucking good. It makes me wonder what the other guys thought they were doing down there before?

All I need is one more minute and I'll find the release I crave. Cas doesn't stop his assault, for which I'm immensely grateful.

Another round of knocking has Cas stopping. Fuck! I'm going to kill someone.

"What?" he yells, keeping himself between my legs. I edge farther down the bed and wrap my legs around his waist, feeling his erection against my thigh. If I can just thrust my hips high enough—

"Thought you'd wanna know, Michael's on his way," Billy hollers back through the closed door.

There's nothing that could extinguish the fire burning in me quicker than the mention of Michael's name. I uncoil myself from Cas and pull the covers over me.

"You definitely should've woken me up last night," I pout.

"Don't worry. I'll make it up to you later," he promises with a wink.

He slides off the bed and begins getting dressed, and with the hope of having multiple orgasms gone, I get up too. Might as well be dressed and ready for when my uncle arrives.

~

By the time Michael strolls into the cabin, we're all sitting around the table, apart from Billy who's sitting out on the front porch. Sparky stayed last night in one of the spare rooms, which surprised me, but not too much.

It feels like a lifetime since I last saw my uncle. He comes into the kitchen and takes us all in, sitting around the table drinking coffee. If I hadn't been scrutinizing him, I would have missed his eyebrow slightly rise before resuming his normal expression.

He was one of the people I desperately missed at college, but now that I know what he did behind my back last year, I want to cry. He still looks the same to me, but everything about him is different. I feel like I don't know this man anymore, and it hurts deeply. Ever since he took me on as his own, he never made me feel like I was a burden, always making sure I had what I needed and wanted. I clench my hands and stab my palms with my nails to keep myself from saying something I shouldn't.

Cas squeezes my knee reassuringly under the table, and I take comfort in knowing he's here.

"Alannah, you're looking well, darlin'," he greets, his voice piercing through the quietness of the room. "Looking good in here too. It needed freshening up."

He holds his arms out for me, but the last thing I want to do is embrace him after what he did to Cas and to me. It must show, because Sparky subtly kicks my foot as he stretches his legs out. Throwing him a glare, I stand and hug my uncle.

"Hey, Uncle Mikey, it's about time you came to see me," I tell him, trying to gather as much enthusiasm as I can.

He sees straight through me. He pulls away and sits me back onto the chair at the table.

"I know you don't agree with my decision, but it looks like it doesn't matter where I put you, the club comes to you regardless." He nods his head at his brothers.

"It doesn't matter. I'm beginning to like it here," I say truthfully. "Is this permanent for me?"

"I'll never ask you to leave here, Alannah. As far as I'm concerned, this is your home now."

He opens his cut and pulls an envelope out from the inside pocket, passes it across the table, and sits in the last available chair. Opening it up, I find cash, and lots of it.

"What the hell is this for?" I ask incredulously. Why the hell would I need all this?

"Now you're here, I'm sure you want to update the place. It could fuckin' do with some modernising. Also, you could buy a setup for you to write again."

Between settling down here, having a bodyguard, and now Cas, I haven't given writing a second thought. I used to sit and write for hours, sometimes poetry, sometimes short stories.

"Maybe," I mutter.

I don't want his money, not really, but I have to be sensible here. I haven't got the stability of living at the club anymore.

"How's Aunt Kitty?" I inquire, moving away from money and his offers of advice.

"She's fine. You'll see for yourself on Saturday." His smile is always bright when he speaks of his wife. It's the only part of him I still recognise.

I'm about to ask him if he could bring her around sooner, but when his phone rings, he holds his hand up, telling me to wait.

Cas and Sparky sit there, listening intently. The mischievous grin on Michael's face tells us all he likes what he's being told. When he ends the call, he shoves the phone in his pocket.

"Come on, boys, Slade's found something. We gotta go," Michael reports, rising from his chair.

"Alannah, if you need anything, call me, or tell the prospect. I'll see you on Saturday."

I suppose I could've asked him why Billy is here, but what's the point? He wouldn't tell me anyway, and if he did, it would only be a lie.

"See you later, Barbs," Sparky says, following Michael out.

I don't have long with Cas, but I'm glad I get to say goodbye—alone.

"I don't know what's going on, but I'll be back later. And I want to take you somewhere," he tells me, pushing me against the wall. My heart rate speeds up so much, I think it will burst out of my chest.

"Where are you going to take me?" I ask breathlessly, as his wicked mouth kisses the most sensitive area of my neck.

"Wait and see."

He kisses me on the lips, squeezes my ass, and is gone.

In the twenty-five seconds we were alone, he had the power to disorientate me to the point I couldn't tell which way was up.

I hear their bikes ride away as I come back to my senses when I hear my phone beep.

I hope it's Bonnie. I hadn't heard back from her yet, and the worry I had before has intensified. Finding my phone on the countertop, I scroll to my messages and groan when I see it's the phone provider offering me a better deal. I haven't gone this long without any contact with her since we became friends. I don't even know where she's from or where she lives, because she's always been evasive when it comes to her personal life.

I sigh. Expecting a full house in a few days, I'd have plenty to do to keep me occupied. Apart from throwing some sheets on the sofa and chairs, the lounge was ready for decorating. May as well get on with it.

Cas

"What do you have?" Michael asks Slade when we arrive at the clubhouse.

Slade's at his spot at the bar on his laptop, where he spends most of his time. If there's anything to be found, he's the guy to find it.

"A Hunter Carson has just acquired himself some property at the edge of town."

Hunter Carson is the President of the Raging Riders. We've never been able to track his property purchases before, as he mostly uses fictitious names.

"Our town?" I ask.

"The one and only," Slade replies, frowning.

"What type of property?" Sparky interjects.

"A warehouse. I've printed off the location and an image of the area. Looks like Dirty Nicky's old place." He hands us the prints.

The Raging Riders' compound is over three hours away from here. He wouldn't need property around here, unless...

"He's planning a fucking patch over," I surmise, feeling sick.

Muttering and curses are thrown around. Sitting on one of the stools, I grab a beer from one of the prospects working behind the bar.

"Over my dead fuckin' body is that going to happen," Michael roars.

"We need to put a stop to this once and for all," I agree.

"Absolutely fucking right we do. Why don't we take out the warehouse along with their clubhouse?" Sparky rubs his hands together, a sinister gleam in his eyes.

It isn't a surprise he would come up with this idea. Any opportunity he gets to play with explosives, he will. It's when he's at his best, and the happiest.

"Do what you need to do and hit them tomorrow night. We'll blow their week well apart," Michael laughs.

Having the go ahead, Sparky is gone in a flash. Michael leaves too, and I disappear to my room. Unlocking and opening the door doesn't feel the same. The bed is still unmade from the last time I slept in it. Beer bottles are littered everywhere, and the laundry that needed to be done days ago is still strewn about across the floor. It's a far contrast from being at the cabin. I step over piles of clothes and eventually make it to the bathroom. Turning on the shower, I get undressed and step under the hot spray of water. It's then I know I don't want this part of my life anymore. I want a home, clean sheets every night, and I want Alannah bent over the washer doing laundry. And most of all, I want a home with her.

Not wanting to be here any longer, I'm out of the shower

and dressed within ten minutes. Grabbing my cut and my keys, I lock my room and head back to the bar.

That's where I find Oak, still propping the bar up. Anytime I see him lately, that's where he is, and I'm beginning to wonder if he's moved, or even went to bed. Checking I have enough time, I go over and take a seat on the stool next to him.

"You okay, old man?"

His response is a grunt as he fills his glass and downs the shot of whiskey.

"What's wrong, brother?" I ask, now worried for my old friend.

"Just reminiscing about the days where we didn't have bullets chasing us. Our only plans were wondering which route to ride, and Michael and I weren't the only originals left. Too much is changing, and I'm not sure if I'm cut out for it," he confides, refilling his glass.

The changes are affecting more than just me. They're slowly eating their way through the club I love so much. The only person who seems to be happy with them is Michael. He's embracing them, once again making my opinion more likely that he is, in fact, up to something.

It makes me more determined to find out what he's hiding and put the club back on the right path.

"We'll have those days back again, brother. I can promise you that," I tell him.

He grunts again, and I know our conversation is over. I slap him on the back before leaving and send a text to Alannah, telling her to be ready soon, and to wear something warm.

By the time I arrive at the cabin, she's waiting on the porch. Remaining on my bike, she makes her way over to me.

"So, where are you taking me?" she asks, full of excitement.

Even fully covered in her tight fitted jeans, boots, and jacket, she looks gorgeous. I have no doubt all the changes in my life I want to make for her are the right ones.

"Thought it was time you were on the back of my bike instead of Sparky's," I smirk, handing over the spare helmet I recently acquired especially for her.

We both know what this means to us without having to say it. I've never had a woman on the back on my bike, and until Alannah, there hasn't been anyone who has come close to getting there.

She clips the helmet in place and climbs on behind me. Wrapping her legs around me has my cock twitching, particularly when she folds her hands so close to my growing bulge.

"Yours is the only one I want to ride on," she giggles in that sexy way she does.

I start the engine before I can change my mind and take her back inside. I've seen how happy she is when she's been on the road, and this is my chance to give that to her, finally. It's also the first time she's left the cabin in a while. Technically, it wouldn't matter to her where we go, as long as she's with me. We have to go quite a ways out to avoid being seen by anyone, but that's no chore for me. I want nothing more than to take her away completely.

I decide to take her to the lakes where I know it would be quiet on a chilly afternoon like today, hence the reason I packed a blanket. I sometimes ride out here when I need a breather from the club and all the shit that's coming with it lately. Over an hour later, I cut the engine by the path that leads down to the lake, grab the blanket and take her hand.

"I know it's cold, but I want to spend time with you away from the cabin and go somewhere like normal couples do," I say, picking a spot by one of the trees.

Sitting down, I lean against the tree trunk and pull her down so she's sitting between my legs.

"I know what you mean. It's so pretty here," she sighs, snuggling against me. Throwing the blanket over us, I wrap my arms around her.

"I never knew this place existed. How did you find it?"

"I was out riding a while back and stumbled across it. I come here sometimes to think."

"And what do you have to think about?"

"All sorts of things. I came here after you left for college a lot. I didn't have to pretend I wasn't thinking about her when I was here and away from everyone."

I can't see her face, but I know she's smiling. Women—all the fucking same. Tell them the truth, which turns out to be a whole lot of sappy crap, and they're mush in your hands.

"I wish I could say the same about you. While I did think of you a lot, it was mainly about how much I hated you."

"How am I doing with that? You still hating on me?"

I have her, we both know it, but the confirmation would be music to my ears.

"You're doing good. Not a lot of hate left now," she teases, raising her head up to look at me.

"Still have some making up to do, huh?"

"I'm not going to say no to your apologizing techniques," she giggles.

Oh, I know how much she likes me making it up to her. It's not all about the sex, though. It's mainly the time I spend with her, doing the normal "couple" things that's breaking down her hate for me. I doubt she any for me now. She just likes me to think there is.

"If I ask you a question, will you answer it this time?" she asks, resting her head against my chest.

Her fingers find their way under my jacket and tee, and brush up and down my bare skin, her cold fingers against my hot skin electrifying.

"Depends what you're going to ask."

"Where are you from? And why do you have two opposing crosses as tattoos?"

She'd asked me this last year, and as I was all for impressing her, not scaring her away, I'd told her I didn't want to talk about it and dropped it.

"That's two questions," I point out. "But I'll answer them both. When I was born, I was left at the doors of a church. The woman, I assume, who left me there, wrapped me up in towels and blankets one winter's night. The sisters named me after an angel. The traditional cross represents how I came into this world and how I was raised, while the upside down cross represents my journey to hell for all the unholy shit I've done, and will most likely have to do in the future."

I wait for her to ask what unholy shit I've done, but she

stays quiet. She knows how shit works in the club. Earning the way we do has certain implications, and the results mainly end in violence and death.

"Do you believe heaven and hell exist?"

"Not really, but if Hell does, I'm prepared for it."

"I don't believe in heaven and hell, so you're safe from burning for all eternity."

"Well, I have nothing to worry about then, do I?" I laugh.

"The only worry we have is telling my uncle about us," she murmurs.

"Let me worry about that."

We sit and talk about everything, and then we sit for a while in silence. Day turns to night, and the stars shine down brightly alongside the moon. It isn't awkward. Neither of us feel the need to talk about anything in particular just to fill the silence.

I comb my fingers through her soft hair and she looks up at me. Her eyes, so deep and open, not only look at me, but right into my soul.

I bend closer and take her lips. She tastes as sweet as honey. It doesn't take long before the kiss deepens, but when her teeth begin to chatter, I decide we need to go.

Rolling up the blanket, we pull ourselves up and head for my bike.

She slides on and squeezes her legs around me, driving me crazy.

"Fucking love you on the back of my bike, babe," I tell her as I tear out of there, ready to get my girl home.

# 8

## Alannah

Last night cemented our relationship and took it to another level.

The peace of having the engine roaring on the road and no one in sight made it feel like we were the only people on the planet as Cas drove us through roads lined with trees on either side. When we stopped, he led me to a spot by the lake and produced a blanket and explained that we both needed the road to unwind after everything that had been going on.

For hours, we talked about anything and everything, but when it got too cold for anything to go further than kissing, we got back on the bike and headed for home.

His body was buzzing with anticipation, as was mine. Instead of jumping on each other as soon as we arrived, he took my hand and led me to my room. Once he removed his boots, and I my shoes, we calmly undressed each other, barely able to contain ourselves from ripping off the clothes that were hindering us from getting to each other's bodies. What turned out to be slow and sensual in the beginning, soon transformed into a desperate need to be as close to the other as possible.

I have no doubts about his commitment to me. The way he looked into my eyes as he caressed my body made me feel like I was the most beautiful girl in the world. His eyes and hands showed me how he felt, and it was the most intense, yet silent exchange I'd ever experienced.

I look at the time and see we hadn't been asleep long. I'm too pumped up to sleep any longer, so I carefully edge my way out of bed and throw on an oversized T-shirt.

Whatever is going on at the club has him looking exhausted, so I leave him to sleep and head down to the kitchen.

Billy must have been awake for a while, because the coffee pot is half-empty and still warm, though he's nowhere in sight.

Opening the fridge, I eye the eggs and sausage, and decide a hot breakfast is in order. One, because I want to cook for Cas, and that's what old ladies do. Secondly, Billy will need all his energy today to decorate the lounge.

Life couldn't be better than it is at this moment.

I'm waiting on the sausages to finish when a pair of strong arms slip around my waist. As I go to twist my head around for a good morning kiss, he claims my neck between his lips.

"I didn't do something right if you're awake already," he chuckles, his breath warm against the back of my neck.

"Trust me, you did everything right, so I thought I'd cook

you breakfast. Go and call Billy in, it's nearly ready," I tell him and twist out of his arms before the sausages burn.

By the time I load the plates, they're both at the table. Nope, life couldn't be better. It's true what Michael said: I wasn't at the club, but the club was with me.

"Where's yours?" Cas asks when he notices I'm not eating with them.

"I'm not hungry yet," I tell him, reaching for my phone off the table.

Still nothing from Bonnie. I send another message asking if she was okay, and to reply as soon as possible.

I keep checking my phone while they eat and talk about the club. Whenever Bonnie replies, it's always within minutes. I sent the message ten minutes ago. Frustrated by her silence, I put my phone down.

"What's going on?" Cas nods to the phone.

"I don't know. My friend from college has gone silent on me," I groan.

"Maybe she's busy."

"Probably," I murmur.

I explain what I think about her home life, how she would return to school bruised and injured in some way, and about the last few messages we shared.

"Don't be worrying yourself. If she wants any help, she'll ask."

He's right. You can't help if it's not wanted.

I type one last message, giving her the cabin's address so she knows where I am if she does need me and leave it at that.

Billy clears his plate, says "thank you" and disappears

again. Cas retrieves his boots and cut and comes back into the kitchen.

"I take it you have to go?"

"Yeah. I got some club business to handle tonight, and I need to go over the details with Sparky," he says, shrugging into his cut.

Club business at night normally means one of two things. Either it's a big deal going down where they want no witnesses around, or an attack.

"When will I see you again?" I immediately cringe at how desperate I sound.

"Probably not until tomorrow. Don't look so worried. I'll be back in one piece," he promises, pulling me into his arms. "Anyway, I want many more nights like last night. I promise I'm coming back to you, okay?" He holds my gaze until I reply.

"Okay."

His mouth claims mine, but before it can turn into more, he releases me and walks out of the room.

I follow him into the hall and stop at the open door, watching him go. His walk is confident and strong—his jeans not too tight, but tight enough you know his ass is as hard as his abs. Climbing onto his bike, he takes his bandana out of his pocket and ties it round his face, keeping only his eyes uncovered. He looks so fucking hot, and he's all mine.

## Cas

The atmosphere is buzzing in the clubhouse when I return. From the messages I got from Slade, everyone's been called in to go to the warehouse with Sparky, and I'm the backup in case anything goes wrong. And from what I can see, they're hyped for it.

Oak is still sitting at the bar, but it's good to see him conversing with Pope. I look around for Slade, but don't see him anywhere. Sparky is busy with one of the club girls, but I don't want to disrupt him. This is his ritual before doing what he does best.

Michael spots me and calls me over.

"All right, boss. We ready for tonight?" I ask as I stroll over to him.

"Hell yeah. Tonight isn't what concerns me, though," he goads, drawing deep on a cigarette.

"Oh yeah? What's wrong?" I make sure to keep my poker face straight. This isn't the time to tell him about my relationship with Alannah.

"Just wondering where my VP keeps disappearing to. You're never fuckin' here anymore." He isn't talking to anyone apart from me, but he's loud enough for everyone to hear, because they pause their conversations and take notice of us.

"Are you keeping secrets from us?" he smirks, as if he knows what secret I'm indeed hiding.

I laugh at his audacity. He has the nerve to question me when there isn't a doubt in my mind he's keeping secrets from us.

"You're fucking questioning me when—" I start before Sparky is at my side, stopping me from saying something I'll regret later.

"Hey, he isn't hiding anything or I'd know about it. He has

a new girl in town. She's got him whipped like you wouldn't believe, Pres," he tells him, trying to laugh it off.

My gaze remains focused on Michael until he backs down. He may not believe what I say, but he wouldn't suspect Sparky of lying to him as well.

"Well, I hope you can live without her tonight, because we can't afford any fuck-ups."

"I'm sure I'll be fine," I snap. I can't stand it when my loyalty to the club is questioned. I've proven time and time again I'll do anything for this club and my brothers, and yet he has the nerve to call me out. I may be lying to him about Alannah, but he has no solid reason for me not to be with her. So until then, he can fuck off.

"Do you still have my back, VP?" he questions.

"As much as you have mine, Pres."

"Come on, brother, I could do with a hand outside," Sparky interjects, pulling me away.

As he pushes me to the door, everyone goes back to their conversations.

"Fuck. I thought we were playing it cool and keeping our eyes open?" he huffs when he sees no one is around. "Every brother in there, including Michael, now knows something isn't right, and you know what happens to a club when there's animosity between the President and his Vice President," he carries on.

"I don't give a fuck!" I shout. "He's up to something, and until I find out what it is, none of us can trust him."

"I know, brother, but we shouldn't be airing our suspicions until we have the fucking facts," he argues. "Come on. I need help loading tonight's party favours."

Later that night, Sparky and I find ourselves sneaking around the Raging Riders recently acquired warehouse. Peering through one of the windows, I don't see anyone around. I don't have a clue about explosives. I'm mainly here as backup for Sparky while he does his thing. Fifteen minutes later, and there's still no Raging Riders around, so we walk back to where everyone is waiting, covering us.

Sparky hands Michael the cell phone being used as the detonator and steps back, while I go and sit on my bike to wait for the blast. As close as this warehouse is to our town, we can't afford to be seen riding away.

"It's ready to go when you are, boss," Sparky beams.

Michael slaps Sparky on the back in admiration, and takes pleasure in pressing down the button on the small cell phone.

The warehouse immediately goes up in one big ball of fire before smaller balls flare up. Eventually, all you can see are flames of fire stretching up toward the dark night sky.

I can't help but cheer and shout with the others at the scene before us. That'll put an end to whatever the Raging Riders have planned here.

"How fucking beautiful is that?" Sparky yells to everyone, proud of his work.

Michael whistles, gaining everyone's attention and signals it's time to leave. We ride the back roads home to the clubhouse to avoid detection, because the beauty of the blast would've been seen and heard all over town.

My brothers pour into the clubhouse to celebrate tonight's

victory. All three of the prospects hurry behind the bar as fists slam down on the bar top, demanding their drinks. The music begins blaring, and as each brother gets their drink, they flee in search of pussy.

I claim one of the empty stools and take the beer being offered by Oak.

"You stand out like a sore thumb," he jokes.

"Huh?"

"You. You're the only one not celebrating," he points out. "You missing this mysterious new girl of yours?" he asks, lowering his voice.

I don't commit to an answer, apart from a slight movement of my head. In fact, I am thinking about the club, but now that he's brought up Alannah—not that he knows she's the mysterious girl—I'm starting to miss her.

"It must be fuckin' love then, young Castiel," he says.

I hate it when they use my full birth name.

"I think you're right."

I've been thinking about it lately, but I haven't voiced these thoughts out loud to anyone.

"I've watched you from the first day you came through the door—what, twelve years ago?" I nod. "You were cocky, arrogant, and because Michael took you under his wing, you knew you were untouchable. You took advantage of your new position and got all the pussy you could get your dick in—" I cut him off.

"Are you getting to a point, old man?"

"If you don't fuckin' interrupt, I will," he snaps. "What I was trying to say is, above the pussy and freedom that was put on a plate for you, you proved yourself as a prospect, as a Lost

Souls member, and most of all, as a man. I was the first one to go against Michael with all that crap last year. I caught you two together when you thought you were alone, and I saw the way you acted around the club. You were different with her, and for that kind of change in a man, it can mean only one thing."

"What has that got to do with it? And what's the point you said you were getting to?" I ask, trying to distract him.

"It has everything to do with it, because I know you ain't been shacked up in town. You've been at the cabin. In the year she was away, if you weren't on a run or working, you were at the bottom of a bottle and face down in pussy. Alannah comes home and you ain't been with anyone here," he concludes.

"If you remember, I took a girl to bed on her first night back."

"Oh, I remember the show you put on, but then I remember hearing the bitch talking to her friend the next day. Guess what I heard?"

He obviously knows about Alannah and me. This is beginning to feel like I'm being tested, again.

He probably heard that I never touched the girl, apart from to hand her two hundred dollars to keep her mouth shut and make out that I fucked her hard if anyone asked. It was meant to pay for her fucking silence. Seeing her sprawled across my bed waiting for me while Alannah was in the same building made me angry, and the thought of touching her repulsed me. But making Alannah hate me that little bit more was so she would keep her distance from me, which made no fucking difference in the end, because it was me who couldn't keep away from her.

"You never touched the girl. You love Alannah whether you admit it or not, and I don't think there's anyone out there I trust more to protect her than you."

Did he just give us his blessing?

"She's like a daughter to me, so if you fuck up and hurt her... well, let's just say—don't."

"I'm not planning on it," I assure him.

"Good. Now, you'd do well to hold off telling Michael. I'll talk to him when things settle down, that's if the ranks don't change and I won't need to."

When he's finished, he turns and sits on the stool beside me and closes himself off.

"What do you mean?"

He takes a healthy swig of his whiskey. "Michael's changing the club, but he might not like the outcome."

He stumbles off the stool and staggers toward his dorm room.

Oak too? At first, I thought it was only Sparky and I that were alone in thinking the club was changing, and from what I see in the way things are heading, it isn't for the better. I wonder how many other brothers feel the same as us?

# 9

## Alannah

The last couple of days have been perfect. Not only considering the pure, unadulterated sex, but also the time spent talking, laughing, and getting to know Cas, both body and soul.

With the rain beating against the window of my room, and the dark clouds making it seem later in the evening than it actually is, it makes our private little bubble appear even more secluded.

The only time the outside world gets through is when Cas's phone goes off. I don't mind, because I know he'll only leave if he really has to.

The last message he received got me worried, though. Apparently, everyone is coming to the cabin a day early. I have enough food and drink for one night, but not two.

Cas assured me they'll bring more themselves so I won't need to leave the cabin.

I'm looking forward to seeing the girls again. I barely saw anyone the night I came home from college, and then I was forced to leave the next morning. I was upset they hadn't been to visit me, but when I think about it, I wouldn't have had it any other way. I've gotten used to being here, and I think if I had the girls around me, I wouldn't have been able to adapt so quickly.

Cas has hinted a couple of times that he's apprehensive about whatever it is going down this weekend. I haven't questioned him about it, hoping he'd tell me, but he hasn't, and this time tomorrow, we won't get a chance to be alone anytime soon. I don't want to be worrying myself over something that might not be that bad.

"What's going to happen on Saturday?" I ask, lying across his chest.

"Destruction and many deaths," he croaks.

I gasp, propping myself up on my elbow. Since Micky, the overwhelming need for the club to be okay when they go off on business is beginning to cripple me.

"As long as it isn't your death," I whisper selfishly.

"I promise. No one can take me out but you, babe."

I'm not stupid enough to believe he'd have a choice in the matter if he was caught in a dangerous situation, but he's careful by nature, and I have to trust him to know what he's doing.

"And once that's over, what will happen to us?"

I need to hear again that I'm not being used just to take all the shit at the club off of his mind, and that we're worth fighting for.

"I don't know, but I can tell you now, I won't do anything to jeopardise losing you."

I believe him, and I trust him. He's mine, and I'm his.

"I love you. I have for a year, and it's why I hated you so much," I blurt out.

I'm not embarrassed to tell him how I feel, especially when his face lights up as he registers what I said.

"I love you too, babe, always have. I just didn't know it until now." Gripping the back of my head, he pulls me down for a kiss.

I tear myself away and speak softly, but with conviction. "So, if you hurt me again, it will be classed as a crime of passion when I kill you," I warn him. It doesn't hurt to drive it home again.

"You're so fucking hot when you're threatening to kill me," he smirks. "Go to sleep. It's going to get busy tomorrow, and I haven't let you sleep much lately."

That's true, so I snuggle against his chest, wondering if I will ever get enough of his body.

He loves me.

I fall asleep with a smile, thinking of how our future is going to play out. I can't wait to find out.

~

I'm disappointed when I wake up alone. Although, once I'm dressed and downstairs, I understand why. Brothers and their old ladies have begun arriving. I spot Billy first, being roped into carrying extra supplies my new guests have brought with them. He grins at me and walks out to help as another truck pulls up. With most of the old ladies here, I'm made useless in the kitchen. They know how to feed their men, and I'm glad I don't have to keep them all fed myself. With everyone settling down and making themselves at home, I answer the door to another guest and find the bitch Danni, who I caught fucking Cas last year, standing before me.

"Oh, hell no," I growl, feeling the anger at her blatant cheek of turning up here.

"Barbie," Sparky drawls out my name in warning, coming up behind me. How is this fair? She's not an old lady!

"She's not staying here," I fume, pronouncing my words very carefully.

I flick my wrist to shut the door in her face, but Sparky quickly puts his foot in the way to stop it. Stepping in front of me, he pulls her through the gap between us and the wall behind him.

"Go and get lost. And whatever you do, stay out of her fucking way," he snarls at her.

Once she runs along in her ridiculously high, cheap heels, Sparky turns on me and shoves me outside.

"You're going to have to squash that jealous shit tonight, Barbs. Michael's all over Cas now, and tonight you're both going to be under his eye." He focuses his sharp gaze on me, making sure I'm listening.

I'm not worried about tonight. I know what I have to do.

"My uncle knows I can hold a grudge. It wouldn't surprise him to see me angry at her still," I argue.

"True, but shit's going down, and none of us need a catfight thrown into the mix."

I punch him on the arm.

"You know I don't catfight," I hiss.

"Well, I know now," he huffs, rubbing his arm. "Come on, you can get me a beer," he grins cheekily.

Throughout the afternoon, everyone busies themselves around the cabin. It's not until night is drawing in that Oak turns up. I didn't realise just how much I missed him until I see him wander into the kitchen. I jump into his open arms and hug him tight.

"Sorry I haven't been to visit, kid."

"That's okay. You're here now." I smile up at him, noting his tired expression. "You okay? You don't look so good."

"I'm good, darlin'. Just getting too old for this shit," he replies.

I grab him his usual bottle of whiskey and a glass as he makes himself comfortable at the table. I sit and catch up with him until Michael and Aunt Kitty arrive.

She seeks me out as she comes into the kitchen. Bustling out of her jacket and dumping her bag on the countertop, she beelines for me and I'm once again embraced in a bone-crushing cuddle.

"Hello, sweetie. You doing okay?" she asks in her soft, angelic voice.

"I'm fine," I assure her.

"I would have come sooner, but I couldn't get a ride here."

She's never had a driver's license, so unless Michael drove her here, or allowed one the prospects to bring her, there was no chance of her visiting.

"Have you been eating properly? You look like you've lost weight," she scolds, giving me the once-over.

"Yes, Aunt Kitty."

"Nope, not good enough. I'll go fix you some dinner."

As everyone is now here, Michael gets the group's attention in the living room.

"Welcome my brothers and family. I hope you've all settled in. Your time here is temporary. Tomorrow night, we have big plans for our enemy, and while we're away, the rest of you will be safe here. So, unleash tonight, because I need you in top fuckin' form tomorrow!" he cheers.

I leave them hooting and howling and sit on the kitchen countertop, watching the old ladies shuffling around like old mother hens. It's a good thing the kitchen is a substantial size, because the men file in too, filling the space wall-to-wall with bodies.

Eventually, the music becomes louder and louder, and the drinks flow. My body reacts immediately when Cas enters the room and takes a seat at the table next to Slade. Sparky brings over a bottle of tequila, lemon slices, and the saltshaker. I know he's trying to keep me occupied while everyone's here.

I neck three shots before I feel the effects start to take over. I'm able to relax. Everyone I love is here, and just for tonight, I'm part of the club again.

"Travelin' Band" just then flows through the speakers. I know what's coming, and so does everyone else, because they move around to the edges of the kitchen to clear some floor space. Sparky's grin grows as the song registers through his alcohol-fueled mind. I'm given no choice. He takes my hand and begins spinning me around. We used to dance to this song every time it came on in the clubhouse when we were younger. We had no idea how to dance to it, but we shuffled our feet and carried out a lot of dips and twirls. Everyone, even Pope in the corner, claps his hands to the beat and joins in. Luckily, the song only lasts a couple of minutes. He twirls me a couple more times, and at the end he dips me so low, I think he's going to drop me on my ass. It doesn't help that I can't stop giggling.

"Okay, I need more tequila if you're going to throw me around," I laugh, escaping back to the tequila bottle. I pour another shot for us, and then wish I hadn't turned around.

Two club whores strut into the kitchen. Jilly—I think her name is—goes over and sits on Slade's lap, while the whore I hate most, Danni, sits on Cas's. I tell myself to keep my cool. I knew this could be a possibility tonight, so I force myself to turn my back on them, neck the shot, and pour another.

"Behave," Sparky growls low in my ear.

"I am," I snap.

I can't stop my heart from beating frantically. Why can't I be in a normal relationship where I don't have to hide how I feel?

After trying somewhat to calm myself, I join the conversations around me again. Well, that is until I make eye contact with Cas and the whore on his lap, who has the balls to give me the dirtiest smirk I've ever seen. Cas is seriously beginning to piss me off too. I understand we have to keep up a pretense, but for fuck's sake, he could at least move her somewhere else. It looks and feels too real, a gut-punching reminder of what I walked in on last year.

Sparky doesn't leave my side. When he feels me losing

control, he asks loudly if I can show him where the firewood is kept.

None too kindly, he shoves me out the back door. The fresh, brisk air hits me, calming me immediately.

"I know what you're going to say," I growl before he can give me a lecture.

"Good. It saves me from fucking repeating myself." Taking my arm in his strong hand, he leads me around the cabin to the front door.

"If it was any other whore, it would be easier to deal with."

"I could tell. It was written all over your face for every brother to see."

"Good thing you got me out of there, then."

Feeling my phone buzz in my pocket, I pull it out to find a message from Bonnie, letting me know she's coming to visit this Sunday. Thank God. I can't wait to see for myself that she's okay.

"Bonnie, my friend from college, is coming to visit this Sunday," I tell him, feeling much better.

"The hot one you roomed with?"

"The one and only," I squeal excitedly. "Don't you scare her away," I warn him.

He holds his hands up in surrender, but the look in his eyes tells me different.

"Come on. Are we going back in or what?"

"I'm not taking you back in there. We'll stay in the lounge from now on," he informs me, opening the front door.

We push our way through the hall, and as we get to the door, I can't help but peek through to the kitchen. I wish I hadn't. Cas isn't at the table anymore, and neither is that whore.

I forgave him for last time because of the circumstances, but tonight is different. He said he wouldn't jeopardize our relationship again for the club, but him disappearing with her sure as hell isn't good. I won't be able to forgive him this time, and he knows that.

I need to be alone. I can't keep this charade up because it hurts too goddamn much. I'm in a room full of people, yet I feel utterly alone.

"I'm going to bed. Wake me up before you go in the morning so I can say goodbye," I tell Sparky, pulling him back so I don't get trapped in the room with someone wanting to speak to me.

He studies me before agreeing, and I escape to my room and collapse against the door in the dark.

I hate that I'm crying. I hate that he's in this house, doing whatever it takes just to keep our relationship a secret from my uncle.

"Lana, I'm here, not there," I hear.

I scan the room and see him walk toward me in the darkness. Sitting beside me on the floor, he puts his arm around me. I can smell her perfume on him and pull away, unable to stand it any longer.

But he's having none of it. He pulls me back in place and keeps me there.

"With everything I've put you through, I knew you couldn't deal with this. Nothing at all happened. I couldn't leave you on your own all night, thinking all sorts of shit. I told you, I'm yours, no one else's."

"Where is she?" I don't particularly care, but if Cas wants Michael to think he's with her and she returns downstairs, he's going to get suspicious real quick.

"I told her I would give her three hundred dollars first thing if she stayed in the room for the rest of the night. And if she doesn't, then I'll make sure she isn't welcome at the club no more. A girl like her needs the club as much as the brothers do," he explains.

I sit up and stare at him. He would do that for me?

"I deserve that look you're giving me, Lana, but please believe me, nothing happened. I love you, and that means something to me."

"I love you too." I lean in to kiss him and sneer, "But you reek of that slut's cheap-ass perfume, and it's making me feel sick."

I get up off the floor and sit at the edge of the bed. Shrugging out of his cut and removing his T-shirt, he tosses them to the far corner of the room and joins me.

I lean against his bare shoulder and sigh.

"Much better. I couldn't think straight. I shouldn't have overreacted like that. I blame some of it on the alcohol."

"I understand how hard this is for you, especially after everything."

"I hate this. We shouldn't have to keep quiet about us."

"I promise, as soon as we get back on Sunday, I'll talk to Michael, and every motherfucker will know you're mine," he tells me, kissing the top of my head.

"You looked sexy as hell shaking your ass earlier. I'll admit, I was jealous you were dancing with a brother and not me."

I roll my eyes at him while climbing onto his lap. Straddling my legs around his waist, I begin kissing the top of his chest.

"No need for jealousy. I'm yours, always."

"Damn right you are, woman."

He falls back on the bed and I follow. Getting rid of my top, I laugh quietly and unbutton his jeans, releasing his already hard cock.

"You're going to have to keep it quiet tonight, baby. Don't want anyone thinking you've got someone in here."

"I'll try."

# 10

## Cas

I left Alannah sleeping just before sunrise. I was right to go to her last night. It broke me to see her collapse to the floor of her room in tears. Knowing my track record caused her to doubt me brought home how much making up I still need to do, and I'm going to everything in my power to gain her full trust again.

I check in on Danni, wanting to make sure she stayed in the room as she was told, and it seems she did. Throwing the cash on the floor by the bed, I make my way downstairs.

Finding an empty chair, I make myself comfortable and try to grab a few hours' sleep. I didn't want to get caught oversleeping in Alannah's room, and there was not a fucking chance I would risk falling asleep in the room Danni's in.

I keep reminding myself that this time next week, I won't be on no fucking armchair. I'll be in bed with my girl, with her soft, warm body sleeping against mine, listening to her little whimpers as she sleeps, and how she always wakes before I do, and wakes me in the most sexual ways.

Fuck. The temptation to go back upstairs and not care about the consequences is too tempting.

I must have drifted off, because I wake up to the sound of people moving about, and a smell that could only mean breakfast is ready.

Through the lounge door, I can partially see into the kitchen, where I find Alannah sitting with Sparky, looking worried. Whatever they're talking about, Sparky seems to say something that puts a small smile on her face before she hugs him and disappears from my line of sight, but returns instantly with two plates of food. Deciding to stretch my legs, I walk into the crowded kitchen, trying not to look at Alannah, and fail. I saw her go to get up but then thought twice. If I didn't know better, I would've guessed she was going to go get me my breakfast. Checking that no one is looking, I give her a sly wink. Her blush turns me on as she lowers her head to hide it.

I can't trust myself to eat with them at the table, so I grab a bacon sandwich and lean against the wall as Michael shows his face.

"Eat up, boys. We're leaving soon."

Kitty whips him up a breakfast plate, and he sits where I desperately want to be—next to Alannah. It's like I'm on the outside looking in, something I haven't felt since I joined the club, and I hate it. I have everything on me I need, and I'd already said goodbye to Alannah last night, so I leave through the back door and escape to my bike.

"Hey, you okay?"

I look around to see Sparky following me out.

"All good, brother," I lie.

"If you hang on a minute, I'll ride with you."

"No, stay. Leave when Michael does, and make sure Alannah's okay," I say, then remember her earlier expression.

"Hey, is she okay? She was fine when I left her, then with you she looked worried."

"She's good. Just worrying we ain't coming home, like Micky. I take it she doesn't know what we got planned?"

"No. She knows shit's going down, but nothing else. Keep it that way, yeah? I don't want her knowing about this shit."

"Sure. I'll see you back at the clubhouse," he replies, jogging back to the cabin.

Tonight better fucking be the end of this. I already feel too old for this shit.

~

After going over the plan again, we bundle into the back of two separate vans and are on our way to the Raging Riders' property.

The effects from the lack of sleep last night are beginning to take over. Their compound is a couple of hours away, so I close my eyes and lean my head against the side of the van. Sleep doesn't come, but the burning in my eyes eases. I listen to Oak and Michael talking quietly opposite me. Sparky sits beside me with his earbuds in, listening to his iPod, while everybody else sits excitedly, anticipating the impending attack.

Stretching my legs as much as I can in the cramped space between us all, I think of what Alannah would be doing now. I know she'll be worried, but luckily, she's got the old ladies to keep her occupied, as well as Billy. A part of me hates she's close to him, and that he gets to spend time with her continuously without being questioned about it by Michael. My ego is big enough to know that she loves me, and wouldn't do anything behind my back.

The sense of knowing she's mine feels intense. Before last summer, I never thought I would let myself feel like this about a woman. To give her the power over me was a concept I couldn't comprehend. To me, women were there to warm my bed on nights I chose, to look good on my arm at parties, and to make me temporarily feel good without having that constant need to please each other all the time. With Alannah, I want nothing more than to spend all my time pleasing her. It feels slightly dangerous giving her that kind of power, but knowing I hold the same over her too, takes us deeper than I could have possibly imagined.

Michael speaking on the phone pulls me from my thoughts.

"Okay... Do you see anyone else?" he asks. I imagine he's speaking to Slade or Pope in the other van.

"Okay, stay where you are. We'll drive up and take a look," he advises before hanging up and sliding the phone back in his pocket.

"All right, everyone, load up just in case. Slade says it's quiet in there, so it looks like no one's home. Sparky, Cas, you know what you've gotta do?" Michael prods.

Sparky searches his bag once more, checking he has

everything. Satisfied, he zips it closed and grasps the handles. Like the warehouse explosion, Sparky and I are going in, and if necessary, everyone will come running with weapons and backup.

Thanks to Slade and his expertise with the computer, we've already found the safest spot for us to sneak through because of the satellite picture he printed off. Michael slides the side door open as we pull our balaclavas down, covering our faces to any potential witnesses—not that we plan on having any. We jump out of the van and run to the side of their compound, stopping by the back fence while Sparky cuts through the wire fencing. I make sure my gun is positioned and follow Sparky as he nips through the hole he's made. Slade was right, the place looks deserted. We're supposed to go no farther than the back of the main clubhouse, hide the bomb somewhere and leave, but with no one here, we both take advantage. Treading carefully in case someone does come out, we edge our way around to the side, and then to the front. Even in the dark, the place is a shithole. There's only a couple of spotlights turned on, so we're mostly in darkness as long as we stick to the side of the building.

"Put it down here," I tell him, wanting this done and finished.

You didn't need to see his grin on his face to know he was excited. You would be able to see it in his eyes from miles away.

I've never understood his fascination for explosions and fire. All I know is Michael took him in after he found him trying to light a fire near one of his warehouses when he was seventeen years old. I don't know what possessed him to trust him. I suppose he saw something in him like he did with me.

I let Sparky do his thing while I scan the area around us. I'd put money on it that there was nobody inside either. It's not what we were hoping for, but it'll send a big fucking message not to fuck with us again.

"Ready. Let's get out of here."

I go back to where he's crouching and pick up his now empty bag, and we make our way back to the van without being seen.

Michael slaps our backs as we climb into the back of the van.

"Done?"

"Your doubt fucking wounds me, boss," Sparky chuckles, handing him another phone.

My adrenaline is pumping. We fucking did it.

"Drive on a bit. Don't want to get caught up in the blast," he laughs.

The van rolls up the road and stops again. Michael opens the side door but doesn't move to get out.

His smile has never been more menacing. Pushing down on the phone, their compound blows apart.

"BOOM!" Sparky roars in delight. "Makes my fucking dick hard."

"I hope there were some of those fuckers in there," Michael muses, more to himself than to us. "Let's go," he tells the driver and pulls out his phone. Calling Slade, he orders him to get the hell out of Dodge.

Our van, as well as theirs, tears out of their pit of a town.

"One hell of a fuckin' warning, boys," Michael grins like a kid on Christmas morning.

Never before I have seen him this hyped for a fight. It's what makes me anxious about him now. He's becoming a loose cannon, and I'm not sure the ending will be what he's expecting. Maybe that's what Oak meant when he babbled on about changes in the club?

"We'll be ready when they next attack. Mark my words, boys, this will all be fuckin' over soon," he promises. Again, it's more to himself than to us.

My chest sinks into my stomach. It was meant to be over tonight.

It's going to be a long ride back to Willow's Peak, and I'm dreading every mile of it.

# 11

## Alannah

Apart from Kitty, Lila, and Jackie, I don't really know the other old ladies. I recognise the club whores, but don't know them personally. They keep to themselves and out of the way, avoiding the old ladies whose men they've slept with, and the old ladies act like they're not here at all.

Danni steers clear of me too, and she's no longer wearing that smirk after being discarded by Cas last night.

Since everyone left yesterday, my heart's been beating frantically, and to my ears, it sounds like an army marching with heavy boots across it. Kitty and the other women are used to their men being away, and use these times to catch up properly with each other. I've spent most of my pacing hours with Billy and the other prospects. Through spending time with him, I found I didn't mind getting to know the prospects.

Jack and Ricky are okay guys. I heard the club whores

having a good time with them last night. If this ever happens again, I will definitely be investing in earplugs.

I find Billy out back at the decking area with a coffee, and join him on the chair.

"You coming out to hide too?" he chuckles.

"Yeah. It feels like we've been invaded, doesn't it?"

He nods his head in agreement and sips his coffee.

"You heard from your friend yet?"

I shake my head. I've been messaging her all weekend, asking what time she'll arrive, and if she needs any help, but she hasn't replied once.

"Have you heard anything?" I ask him.

It's not normal practice for a prospect to be kept in the loop with this sort of club business, but I'm hoping Cas might have sent him a message of some sort.

"Only that they're on their way back, and they want their women to leave as soon as they arrive."

What? That doesn't sound right.

"How long before they get here?"

As soon as I ask, we both hear engines approaching around the front of the cabin.

"About thirty seconds," he jokes.

"Ha-ha," I mutter, standing to go and wait in the kitchen.

I have butterflies. Proper schoolgirl, first crush butterflies. My nerves are shot to pieces wondering who was coming home, and who wouldn't be walking through the door. It's been the longest weekend of my life.

I sneak in through the back and keep close to the door, watching closely as brothers file into the kitchen, going to their women or taking seats at the table, all stone-faced and tired. No Cas yet. Sparky's next through the door, and I cross the kitchen to hug him with everything I have.

"Where is he?" I whisper close to his ear.

"He's good, Barbie," he whispers back.

As soon as he tells me this, I see Cas walk through the front door. He stops when he sees me and smiles before carrying on and entering the kitchen.

They're home, they're fine, and most of all, we can tell Michael about our relationship.

I thought it would be my luck Bonnie would show up now and be scared away by all the bikers. I check my phone quickly while Michael was speaking with Kitty. Still nothing from her.

Most aren't sticking around, taking their old ladies with them. Jack and Ricky leave with the club sluts, thank God.

Kitty wraps me in her arms, promising to come and visit me more, then heads out with Michael and Oak, leaving Sparky, Slade, and Cas.

"Is your friend here yet?" Sparky asks, wiggling his eyebrows.

From the corner of my eye, I see Cas look at me in surprise. Oh yeah, I forgot to tell him the other night. To be fair, I did have other things on my mind.

"No. She messaged me saying she'd be here today, then nothing. She's not replying, and she's not taking my calls," I frown.

For weeks I've felt she's in trouble, and the more I think about it, I feel justified in worrying.

"I'm sure she's fine. Anyway, let me know when she gets here," he grins.

"You're not going to touch her, Jason," I warn him.

"Are you making it a challenge?" he teases.

"No, I'm making it a promise."

He only laughs as he walks out, with Slade following behind him.

"Hey, Slade. Wait." He turns as he's about to open the door.

"What's up?"

"Can you do something for me?"

"Depends when. I've had a long night and I need some sleep."

"It doesn't matter when," I tell him quickly. "Can you find out where my friend lives, and see if you can find anything on her please?"

"Sure. What's her name?"

"Bonnie Hamilton."

"I'll let you know what I find."

"Thank you. Now, go and get some sleep."

I don't know why I didn't think to ask him to do this before.

Walking back into the kitchen, I feel the butterflies flutter around again. We're finally alone.

I sit on his lap and he holds me tight. He's really okay. I crush my lips against his, showing him just how happy I am he's home, and he responds instantly, gripping my hips as I grind myself against his erection. I moan into his mouth, and then we're moving when he stands and places me on the countertop. Our lips hardly left each other's as I shimmy out of my shorts while he undoes his jeans. They barely hit the floor before he's pushing into me.

This is hard, fast, and raw. With each thrust tipping me over the edge, I cling to his cut and take everything he gives me.

"I'm not going to last much longer if you keep clenching that sweet fucking pussy of yours," he growls.

"I'm not going to last much longer anyway," I pant.

The kitchen becomes a blur as he carries on, pounding relentlessly into me and I cry out, reaching my climax. He thrusts into me twice more before he finds his own release and stood shaking, gripping my chin.

"I needed you so fucking bad," he breathes, kissing me again.

"I know how you feel. You don't have to go too, do you?"

"I ain't going anywhere, baby." His smile melts me all over again.

## Cas

Sitting up against the headboard, with Alannah sleeping beside me, I now have time to digest and run through last night's events. Blowing up their warehouse was a big fucking statement, and the repercussions are going to be just as dire. I used to welcome a fight. Going after the Raging Riders would've been my only priority. It would've been my mission to bring them all down just for the fact of disrespecting my club and continuing to do so. If I got taken out, I would've done it with a smile on my face, knowing I'd gone down fighting, always loyal to my club.

Now I'm fiercely loyal to my girl as well, and the thought of being taken out and leaving her alone terrifies me.

In an ideal world, I would have the club, my girl, and ride the road far and wide. The only thing at my back would be Alannah, with her blonde hair blowing in the wind. When I imagine it, it makes me hungry for it, but now there's always bullets chasing us, and the ghosts of our enemies cackle in my ear. Feeling like we're not making progress is beginning to take its toll, and not just on me, but on the whole club. The more I think about it, the more I feel like last night was an unnecessary risk. I can't understand why Michael wants to put us in danger, because that's where we're at. And if I have to choose to protect the club or Alannah, she's going to win every fucking time. Alannah is as much a part of the club as me or any other brother. Her pure light brightens the dark pit that is the world we live in.

I don't think she comprehends that she's mine in every way and always will be. To go back to a life she isn't a part of would be destructive to everyone and everything around me. My heart pounds in my chest just thinking about it. No, she's mine, and to prove it to myself, I hold her closer to me.

This girl is the only reason I want better for me, for us, and for the club. To have better, we need to be clever. Blowing up shit is only going to end with neither club having any property. At the time, I thought it was a good idea, but now I'm not so sure.

Cautiously leaning over the bed, I pull my phone from my jacket pocket. My right hand is trapped around Alannah, so to keep from waking her, I spend an extra five minutes typing a message left-handed to Slade, telling him to go over all the information we have on the Raging Riders, and to dig deeper using his super hacking skills to see if he can find something new we can use. We have to be missing something. They can't evade us forever.

I drop the phone to the floor, position myself against my girl and fall asleep.

# 12

## Alannah

No contact from Bonnie and nothing from Slade couldn't even distract me from Cas, who hasn't left since the club returned home on Sunday. He'd told me most of the brothers were taking a few days off with their families, and since I was his, this is where he's staying.

Billy has been disappearing often, as Cas and I haven't been able to keep our hands off each other. Trying not to think about the sex—and trust me, there's been a lot of it—it's the normal, simple, everyday tasks that are making me the happiest. Cooking together, lying on the sofa watching trash on TV while he soothingly strokes my hair, and the way he makes sure the cabin is secure every night. Exactly what a man of a house does for his family.

The last few days have been quiet and uninterrupted, until today. Every member has been called in for church. Cas assures me he hasn't been told of any comebacks as of yet, and not to worry. I'm trying not to, and up until Micky, I hadn't before. The guys are proper men who take care of business. Hopefully, in time, my nerves won't dance on edge every time they leave to deal with whatever.

Me in bed and Cas in the shower, I eye his jacket and bandana draped across the back of the chair. Slipping out of bed, grab them both and quickly jump back under the warm sheets. Listening out to make sure the water is still running, I unfold the bandana and wrap it around my chest, fastening it to give me extra cleavage. It works well with my black panties. As I hear the water cut off, I slip into his jacket and kneel on the edge of the bed. When he comes into the bedroom in nothing but his towel, his chest glistening from water beads, he stops dead in his tracks—his eyes wide, his mouth agape.

"You sure I can't tempt you to stay?" I purr, trying to be seductive.

His dick promptly stands at attention, tenting the towel. He doesn't answer, but within three strides he's on top of me. I'd done well. He loves what he saw, because he fucks me senseless with them on, and doesn't let up until he's coming inside of me.

"Fuck, Lana. Every time I wear this, all I'm going to think is your tits are on my face."

I giggle into his chest, feeling proud of my creative efforts.

"Good."

"You're going to fucking kill me, baby."

"That's not my plan. I'm not finished with you yet," I smirk.

"You'll never be finished with me, but right now, I really

have to go." Reaching behind me, he pulls at the knot in the bandana.

"So fucking hot," he mumbles, getting off the bed.

My phone beeping startles me. No one apart from the phone company and Bonnie has contacted me, so I jump up, hoping it's Bonnie.

*Sorry I'm a few days late, but I'll be there in half an hour.*

I jump up and down excitedly. She's actually coming, and you can bet your ass she'll be explaining what's been going on with her lately.

I snatch a fresh pair of jeans, top, and underwear from my drawers before making a beeline for the shower.

Cas catches my wrist as I pass him on my way to the bathroom.

"What's with the rocket up your ass?"

"That was Bonnie. She'll be here in half an hour," I squeak.

His frown dampens my spirits. What does he have to frown about? It's not like I won't be spending time with him too, especially when we're alone at night.

"What?"

"How are you going to explain having Billy here?"

I think quickly. "I'll tell her he's my cousin visiting from out of town. Cas, I can't wait for you to meet her. She's so sweet... and don't be telling Sparky she's coming. Otherwise, we won't get rid of him."

"How does he know her?"

"If he was on a run or close by, he would visit me at

college. He met her a couple of times and flirted with her, but she was pretty timid around him."

"He visited you?" he asks quietly.

"You didn't know that?"

He shakes his head. "I would've visited you at every opportunity if I could have," he offers sadly.

"Hey, I'm here now, and so are you," I assure him, standing up on my tiptoes to kiss him.

"I know. Okay, babe, I'll be back tonight. Stay indoors. Make up some shit if to your friend if she wants to go into town."

"I will."

After one last kiss, he leaves, and I jump in the shower.

~

Entering the lounge, I find Billy. I don't know when this happened, but there's now a game console hooked up to the TV. I stand by the window on lookout for Bonnie, telling him about her coming today, and that he's to pretend he's my cousin. He quickly agrees before turning his attention back to his game.

"I hope she arrives soon. It's beginning to rain," I say, gazing out of the window.

This gets Billy's attention. "I should get the truck in the garage. She can be temperamental in this weather and the back window has been smashed in."

"I'll get some dinner on while we wait," I tell him, following him out of the room.

I make a mental note to go shopping soon. The fridge is

beginning to look bare, I think, dumping chicken and vegetables onto the counter.

I hear too many cars... no, wait... are those van doors being slammed shut? I walk through to the hall and am greeted with Billy being thrown through the front door. I scream as the panic begins setting in at seeing bikers who aren't Lost Souls fill the doorway. I run for the stairs, and halfway up I turn, hoping Billy's behind me. He's not. He's literally being jumped on by two men—big, fat, dirty biker men. Within seconds, his face is covered in blood. I scream again, and Billy's head whips around, focusing intently on me before one of the men's boots connects with his ribs.

He mouths 'Go' before his eyes squint closed in pain.

What the fuck is going on? These aren't the bikers I grew up with.

I run the rest of the way to my room, but if Billy thinks I'm going to hide, he's wrong. I mentally kick myself for not going to the stash of weapons in the hall, and then remember Cas moved one of the guns to my room. Finding it under my bed, I check to make sure it's loaded with shaky hands. Getting a grip, I turn to go when two different men to the ones I first saw burst into my room.

I know this is about survival, and not just mine, but Billy's as well. Without hesitation, I aim and shoot. One man goes down, and I quickly aim and shoot at the second. Being much closer, I feel his blood spray over my face, land on my hands. I don't give myself time to think about it and run to the stairs where the two fat men are still pummeling into Billy.

I scream at them until I'm at the bottom step. Pointing the gun at them, I scream for them to stop.

I'm not big and burly, or muscular and tall, but them laughing at me pushes my anger to levels I never knew existed.

"Don't be a fuckin' stupid bitch. Put that down," one of them growl.

My eyes dart to his patch before holding his glare. He's the President of the Raging Riders.

Fuck.

"Get away from him," I sneer.

"Who, him?" he laughs, kicking Billy in his lower back.

"Leave him alone!" I scream, taking a step toward him. When the second biker comes forward, I jump back on the step.

"Look at your hands shaking. You ain't shooting shit," the president sneers.

I tense my hands, trying to calm down, but it only makes it worse. I look to Billy, who's losing a lot of blood—too much. I look between Billy and the men, praying they'll leave, or that we'll get out of this somehow alive.

"I can't believe those cunts let their women play with guns," biker two growls.

"Shoot them," Billy chokes out, spitting up blood.

"Shut the fuck up!" the President shouts, kicking him repeatedly.

My first reaction isn't to shoot him, but to throw the gun down. I scream for him to stop until my throat is raw. It feels like a nightmare I sometimes have, where I'm trying to scream but no sound comes out. The throbbing in my throat tells me I'm screaming, but it's like they can't even hear me.

It registers what I've done when he finally lays off of Billy and nods to Biker Two for him to get me.

He steps forward, and bless my friend, beaten to a bloody mess, summons enough strength to get up and try to block the biker intent on grabbing me. It all happens so fast. The President pulls Billy away and throws him into the wall. I cry out as I can't do anything but watch him slump to the floor. I scream even louder when I see he isn't moving.

My friend is most likely dead on the floor in front of me, all because I didn't shoot them.

"Shut her up," the President snaps, hovering over Billy's body.

I feel a hand fist into my hair, and the next thing I know, I'm being swung around, my head slamming into the wall.

It fucking works—I shut up immediately. The shock of what he did scares me silent. He doesn't loosen his grip as he pulls me by my hair out to their van. Another biker opens the side door and I'm thrown inside. Through my tears, I can see the President still laying into Billy's body with his big, black boots. If he wasn't dead before, he will be now. No human body could sustain those injuries and recover.

He finishes murdering my friend and joins us at the van, when another biker comes running up behind him.

"Pres, bitch must've killed Slug and Larry. There's no one else in the house," he tells him.

His face contorts into the most horrific expression. What's more, his silence makes him more terrifying.

The last thing I see is his fist flying toward my head as he leans in toward me.

Everything goes black.

# 13

## Cas

I park my bike in the garage at the compound and check my phone. Twenty missed calls from Slade. What the fuck?

I jog across the compound toward the clubhouse. The rain that's begun falling on the way back has stopped, thank God.

Once again, it looks like I'm the last one here. My eyes dart to Slade's usual spot at the bar, where he's sitting without his laptop, and in its place is his phone. Mine begins ringing again, his name flashing across the screen. I hit decline and walk over to him.

"Why are you burning up my phone, brother?" I ask, leaning on the bar next to him.

"Why the fuck haven't you been answering your fucking phone?" he barks, his voice booming across the room.

"I was on the road, coming here," I huff, a bit taken aback

by his attitude toward me. "Care to explain what your problem is?"

"The other day, Alannah asked me to check her friend out." I presume he's talking about Bonnie.

"I guess she was worried about her. Anyway, it took some digging because her last name is different. None of us would've known. All that time she was at college right under our noses..."

He's babbling, so this can't be good. My mouth goes dry in anticipation.

"And...?" I urge him.

"She's Hunter Carson's daughter," he mumbles, immediately following up by necking the rest of his beer. "I called you because I ain't stupid. I know when you're not here, you're with her."

What were the chances of her being roomed with Alannah? Both MC brats— rival MC brats at that?

"It's a good thing Bonnie flaked on her. You should tell Alannah not to have anything to do with her."

I pull out my phone to call her, and it hits me.

"Fuck! Fuck! Fuck!" I yell.

"What?" Slade storms, jumping off the stool.

"It's too late. Lana got a text before I left saying she was a half hour away."

"Hunter's daughter is on her way to our Alannah's place?" he asks, wanting to make sure he heard correctly. "Oh, this is not fucking good... not good at all."

I frantically call Alannah's phone—no answer.

I frantically call Billy's phone—again, no answer.

Fuck taking this to the table. There's not one explanation

that I can begin to think of for this Bonnie bitch to make friends with my girl. I would lay my life on the line and say she was being used, and has been for a long time.

I face my brothers, half of them already looking at us, and call out for quiet. Michael comes in looking put out, wondering what's going on.

"Slade's brought some shit to my attention. While Alannah was at college, she had a roommate, and I've just found out that she's Hunter Carson's daughter," I tell them all.

They begin muttering, all looking confused.

"This can't be a coincidence, not with the Raging fuckers. And, I know for a fact this bitch is on her way to the cabin, if she ain't already there."

"Well, let's fucking go," Sparky roars, coming to stand in front of me, every man in the club buzzing with anger behind him.

I wouldn't fucking ask them to go, because I don't need to. All loyal to my girl, they'll follow, no questions asked.

I fucking love them for it.

I hadn't spoken the words, but none of my brothers are stupid. They know she's my old lady, and it's Michael coming between us.

I hold Michael's stare for a full minute before he nods and joins us as we leave for our bikes.

~

The ride to the cabin is torture. Hopefully the bitch didn't turn up. But if did, we would find them hanging out and gossiping. Damn it. I better find her unharmed, sitting on the fucking sofa.

None of us truly expected what we see when we pull up to the cabin.

No unfamiliar cars. The front door is hanging off its hinges, smears of blood all down the porch steps, and our prospect slowly dragging himself across the gravel toward his truck. It looks like something out of a horror movie. He's so messed up he's unrecognisable, covered in so much blood.

I'm off my bike in a shot and running to Billy. Everywhere is quiet—too quiet. Feeling sick, I swear loudly, dropping to the ground next to him.

"Pope, Oak, get in the house and find Alannah," Michael orders, joining me next to Billy.

"She's... not... here," he splutters, blood spewing from his mouth with each word he speaks.

He has to be in an unimaginable amount of pain, but I need to know what happened.

"Billy, tell me what went down," I plead.

Every one of my weaknesses are on show. They're written on my face, and can be heard in my shaking voice.

"Told her...to go...she came...back...didn't shoot...them."

Shoot them? She knows her way around a gun for sure, but it's not who she is.

"How many were there?" I ask, frantic for more information.

"Too many... just me... she... gave herself up... for me."

That's not hard to believe. We'd all told her she was going soft.

"Raging fuckers... got her... I couldn't... save her," he splutters through more blood.

"Okay, okay. I get it, man. We'll get you to the Doc. You'll be fine," I lie. I don't believe he'll live to see another day. I've seen some sick shit in my time, but this is just too fucking much.

"I'm sorry... get her... back."

"You gave us everything we need. Try not to talk now, brother," I urge him.

He smiles, showing his bloodstained teeth.

"Brother," he whispers.

"Your loyalty to my girl has cost you your life. One man, or God knows how many, you never stood a chance. You're dying a Lost Souls brother."

There's no point in trying to hide his fate from him at this point. We all know he stands no chance of surviving the night.

He chokes on his blood one last time before his head rolls to the side of my arm.

Choking on my own fear, I place him back on the gravel and stand, staring at the sky.

"Michael, you better get your ass in here," Oak shouts from the upstairs window.

I'm running before Michael, and find Oak in Alannah's bedroom.

Cold on the floor are two Raging Rider fucks, dead. One has a bullet in his skull, and the other has one in his chest. Why the fuck didn't they take their dead with them?

I drop to the floor and check under the bed, the gun I left

there for her is gone. I knew my girl could shoot, but her aim under pressure was out-fucking-standing.

Sparky is the first to speak as he checks their patches, while everyone else stares at their bodies.

"She managed to get rid of Larry and Slug, Hunter's VP and nephew," he whistles.

"That ain't good for her. Hunter's going to be out for her blood now. Him and his VP go way back," Slade relays.

I can't handle this anymore. I lash out, kicking and punching anything I make contact with. When that's not enough, I start kicking the lifeless pieces of shit on the floor. Sparky and Oak pull me out onto the landing, and when I see Michael leave the room, I round on him, not giving a fuck if he knows about us anymore.

"This is your fucking fault!" I shout. "You used a fucking poor reason to put her here and made yourself feel better by leaving a prospect."

"Calm down, Castiel," he warns.

"Fuck off. If she doesn't come back, then neither do you."

I'm not fucking about with threats either. He understands it's a promise.

The brothers out on the landing gasp audibly.

"Listen, Cas," he snarls, raising his voice. "If she has her phone on her, we can track her," he informs us. Without thinking why he would go to the trouble of having her bugged, I turn to Slade.

"Search the place. See if her phone's here."

He disappears down the stairs while I shrug out of Sparky and Oak's grip.

No one moves as I get into Michael's face.

"You have my loyalty and my blood when it comes to the club and my brothers, but I'm telling you now, Lana's my old lady, and I'm going to kill anyone who gets in my way of bringing her home."

He swallows hard and nods.

Until Alannah's home in my arms and every fucker who had a part in taking her is dead and in the ground, I can't give a fuck about club ranking. She's my woman, and I'll say how it goes down when it comes to getting her back.

I would've expected the others to speak up, but as I look from brother to brother, they remain silent, giving me their loyalty with nods all around.

"Pope, Oak, you two take care of the bodies. Their blood is on Lana, and I don't want any of this shit to come back on her. Then take our brother Billy back to the club."

They both agree and leave as Slade comes up the stairs.

"Her phone ain't here," he huffs, noticing the difference in the air around us.

"That's good. Get to the club and get on that fucking machine of yours. Find her."

He leaves, and everyone else remains, waiting on me to give them orders.

"The rest of us will head back and call every brother in the fucking area. We're going to war, and we're not coming back until they're all dead in the fucking ground."

# 14

## Cas

Four hours and three minutes have passed, and we're no closer to finding Alannah than we were at the cabin. Slade sits vigilantly at his laptop, waiting for a signal to appear. Michael disappeared into his office as soon as we got back, while the rest of us pulled every weapon we had. Luckily, Sparky thought to bring the stash from the cabin too.

For the past hour, brothers from other chapters slowly arrived and were filled in on what had happened.

Not only is Alannah my old lady, she's been an important person in these men's lives. She doesn't need her family connection to the club. Looking around, I feel the respect and love they have for her.

I can't get Billy out of my head. I got to thinking, even if two or three Raging Riders showed up wanting to take her, he still wouldn't have survived. I desperately wanted to blame him, but I couldn't. But it's someone's fault, and when I find out who, they're going to wish they'd never laid a finger on what's mine.

My body is aching from head to toe. I've been punched, kicked, even stabbed a couple of times, but none of that amounts to the pain I feel now at the thought of losing her.

Hunter's nickname comes to mind—"Noose", as in his preferred method of taking someone out by watching them hang. Sometimes he makes it quick by positioning his victims so their necks snap instantly on impact. Other times, he likes to watch them suffer, drawing their deaths out for hours, even days.

"I've got a signal!" Slade shouts to everyone.

About fucking time.

Staring at the laptop screen, it looks like she's at a warehouse, and not one I recognise.

"It's roughly a two-hour drive north," he informs us, tapping on the keys a mile a minute.

"Okay, you heard him. We've got a location," I call out loudly. Everyone falls silent and I carry on.

"Alannah's my old lady. Most of you have known her all her life. She's our family, and you all know what happens to fuckers who mess with that. Take out any fucker who gets in your way. Get in quick and get her out even quicker," I tell them. "All prospects will join us. The more men we have, the better," I add.

They all look to Michael, who nods, and they look back to me.

"Anyone have a fucking problem?"

They all shake their heads and remain silent.

"We leave now. Get your shit and hit your bikes. Everyone from the mother chapter will go in the vans."

I'm on the edge, and it's taking all I have to keep it reined in.

"And tonight, brothers, this ends. I don't want a Raging Rider fuck left alive by the time we're finished."

Ending my speech, the clubhouse vibrates with their roars and vengeance for blood.

We're sixty men strong. The amount of bikes will be hard to hide, but until Alannah's safe, I couldn't give a fuck. We need to make an impact, and this is it.

I grab the duffle bag I'd packed full of guns and ammunition and head outside. Sparky's already waiting by one of the vans, so I make my way to him and throw my bag in the back.

"The prospect was alive when we got there. Barbie will still believe he's alive. For some reason she took to him. This will crush her, and I know her well enough to know she'll blame herself for his death," he says, stubbing his cigarette on the ground under his boot.

"She's not to blame, Michael is. He's the one who put him there, and I'm going to make sure she fucking knows it."

I couldn't console her over Micky's death, but I'll be damned if I won't be by her side until her tears run dry and she's smiling again.

"Cas, hang on."

Michael comes jogging over. Nodding to Sparky, he turns and jumps in the van.

"You've shown some impressive leadership skills tonight."

I want to tell him to shut the fuck up. I'm not trying to

show off my skills. I'm doing it without thinking, and doing it for my girl.

He holds up his hand to shut me up.

"When we get back, I won't stand in your way with Alannah. I don't think I'll meet another man who'll run out, guns blazing, to end a war over a woman. Tonight, this is going to be the end," he promises.

All I've wanted is his blessing, and now I have it, it feels wrong. It feels planned.

Whatever it is, I don't have time for some heart to heart bullshit right now, so I nod and get in the van.

Forty-three roaring bikes and two vans crammed with seventeen men ride out of Willow's Peak.

~

We've been on the road for an hour, the tension growing. The closer we get, the more you can taste the violence that hangs in the air. We stay mostly silent, preparing ourselves for the fight of our lives to come.

Loading and unloading my gun keeps my hands and mind busy, until like a fucking jigsaw being put together at lightning speed, a thought speeds through my head.

Everything is beginning to add up. Michael going to the extreme, threatening to rip my patch from me, then forcing Alannah out of the club and into the middle of nowhere, claiming she wouldn't be living our lifestyle anymore, but still keeping her close and a prospect by her side. If he truly wanted Alannah out of the club and away from our world, he would've sent her far away, and on her own. Continuously warning me away, calling me out in the club about my disappearing acts, like he was trying to keep her isolated. He knew if she was with me, I wouldn't let her out of my sight, and she definitely wouldn't be living in the middle of nowhere.

And thinking back through today, he's remained calm and collected throughout. He's her uncle, her blood, taking her on as his own. He should've been livid. He should've put me in my place, overriding my relationship with his niece and took charge, but he let me continue to give out the orders, and even praised me for it.

And most of all, why have her tracked if she wasn't to be a part of the club anymore?

Like a ton of fucking bricks falling on me at once, it hits me. No, there's no way he would do that.

I vibrate with anger, barely able to hide it. I load my gun for the final time and slowly raise my arm, pointing it straight at Michael's head.

There wouldn't be a single person in this van who wouldn't be covered in brains and blood at such close range.

"What the fuck, Cas?" Sparky snaps, ripping his earbuds out.

I couldn't tell you what the brothers' faces are showing. My eyes are trained on Michael's.

"One more time. Why did you force Alannah to the cabin?" I question, keeping my voice calm.

He shows no fear. His arrogant features have me nearly pulling the trigger without waiting for his answer.

"I think you know. Otherwise, you wouldn't be pulling that gun on me, son," he replies quietly.

"I don't want it to be true," I whisper.

He's been a father figure to me since the day he first caught me trying to steal a car, but what he confesses will change everything.

"Will someone tell us what the fuck is going on?" Sparky shouts, looking between the two of us.

"Are you not going to deny it?" I ask, my voice pleading, hoping I'm wrong.

"No."

"Okay, I'm going to shoot you both if you don't fucking tell us what's going on," Sparky growls low.

"He used Alannah as bait."

# 15

## Alannah

Coming back to reality isn't pretty. I'd rather have stayed wherever I was in knocked out land. My head hurts like fuck. Not only do I have the headache from hell, I'm hanging from sort of contraption in the middle of a warehouse. Trying to gain my bearings, I can't see much. There are a couple of lights on, with one of them shining on me, making it difficult to see farther than the glow around me.

It's freezing, and the air smells like rain and dirt. I don't know how long I've been here, but I hope Cas returned to the cabin and found Billy. I knew he was gone. Oh God, I remember him slumped on the hallway floor... No, I can't think about him, not yet. I have to focus on myself, and how I'm going to get out of here.

My hands are tied above my head to a chain, and I'm

standing on crates. My arms ache from the pressure, and when I notice a rope around my neck, I look up and see it tied around a rafter. What the fuck? Am I going to be hanged? Who the fuck does that?

I take a better look at the contraption I'm tied to, thinking I have it figured out. My hands are tied to a chain that keeps me in place. The chain is connected to the rope somehow, so if anyone kicks the crates out from under me, I'll hang. When I try pulling my arms down, the rope around my neck tightens. I have no chance of getting myself free.

I don't have much time to think about anything, as a door on the far side opens, and the two men from the cabin walk through.

"Ah, our guest is finally awake," the President says joyfully.

He comes into the light, giving me a better look at him. I didn't take any notice of his looks earlier, what with attempting to save Billy.

He looks about the same age as my uncle, but his hair is much more speckled with grey. His beard is longer than most, and I swear if I got any closer, I would see the dirt buried in it. He's tall, and maybe one day long ago he had muscle, but he just looks fat now, his belly protruding and round. I doubt his cut would reach far enough around to do up. Most of all, he's just dirty.

He steps closer toward me and tugs on the rope above my head. I feel the squeeze around my neck, and fear like I've never experienced before blows me apart from the inside out.

"Just checking you're comfortable, bitch," he sneers.

Since he's this close to me, I spit in his face.

"They'll be coming for me, and they'll kill you for this!" I scream.

He wipes his face with the back of his hand and wipes it on my top, using extra pressure as his hand runs over my breasts.

"I want them coming for you, but those pussy bitches won't be doing nothin' but dying. We're waiting, we're ready, and when they come, we're going to blow each and every head off of those motherfuckers."

No. I'm not going to lose anyone else to these animals.

I laugh at him, using every ounce of strength I have left to show his threats aren't scaring me, because on the inside, I'm full of fear.

"We've been watching you. Baffled us at first why you were out in the middle of nowhere, but we got over it and used that to our advantage in the end. Saw that cunt Castiel making himself at home in your pussy and knew you were special. Not only that fuckin' prick Michael's niece, but the VP's old lady too. Don't get much better than that. The pussies think they can blow up my shit and get away with it? You're fuckin' wrong, bitch. When they get here, they'll die. If you play nice, I'll let you watch as I rip your uncle's throat out," he laughs.

Biker Two hasn't moved or said a word. He just stands there, watching, agreeing with everything his president says.

"Oh, how rude of me, we haven't been introduced. I'm Hunter Carson. No need for your name, bitch. I know all about you. Have for a long fuckin' time."

Funny, the way he keeps calling me bitch, I would think that's my name.

"Fuck off, I don't need to know your name. I won't

remember it when my club puts you in the ground," I tell him, hoping and praying I'm right. If not, then I'll die, and if I'm going to die, I'm not going to give them the satisfaction of seeing me crumble.

"Your club?" Biker Two chuckles. "No wonder the cunts don't know their heads from their asses. Their women have too much fuckin' say."

"Feisty, ain't she?" Hunter grins. "If my daughter was as feisty as you, I might have given her more leeway. Fuckin' disgraceful mistake she was," he mumbles to himself.

"Having you for a father, I'm not surprised she isn't feisty." He's probably beaten the shit and any feistiness she had out of her.

Oh God, why can't I stop goading him?

"Stop talking now, bitch," he warns.

"I'm not a bitch, and fuck you."

Oh please, Alannah, stop, I tell myself.

My stubbornness gains me a back-handed slap. My lip splits on impact, filling my mouth with blood and dripping down my chin. Somehow, I still manage to let out a small giggle. If I ever imagined I would be kidnapped and tied up, I would've thought I'd be scared shitless, but from somewhere, and God knows where, I dig deep, determined not to show any weakness.

The sound of my giggle sends him over the edge. Gripping my chin with one hand, he fists the other and smashes it against my head once, twice, three times. My vision blurs and I almost black out, my skull bouncing around until he finally stops.

I can feel the blood running down my forehead, and

when it flows over my eyebrow and into my eye, my vision goes red.

I can't focus on one single thing. He begins taunting me again, telling me how my club is going to die painfully while I watch, and how I'm going to die if they didn't turn up soon. He yanks my hair back, placing his face next to mine. It takes me a minute to focus, and I think I see Biker Two in front of us, holding up a phone. Is he taking a picture?

I have too much blood in my mouth. Turning my head to the left, I spit all I have at Hunter, painting his cheek in blood and spit. Releasing my hair, he then grips my mouth. My lip throbs as more flows out.

"Michael, Castiel, you better hurry up. This bitch can't keep her fuckin' mouth shut. If you want her alive, you better ride faster, boys," I hear him say. Who the hell is he talking to?

I manage a "fuck you" before my vision completely clouds over, and I'm back in knocked out land.

# 16

## Cas

"Michael? Tell me the kid's wrong," Oak hisses, speaking for the first time.

I still haven't taken my eyes off him, nor has he.

"I had to do something," he replies weakly.

It's all the admission I need.

"Prospect, stop the van," I order.

No sooner does the van stop, Oak has the back doors open, and I'm shoving Michael out.

I jump out and carry on, pushing him to a patch of grass on the side of the road. The others begin stopping and parking up along the stretch of road and joins us to see what's happening.

My final push to Michael's back sends him to his knees. I walk around him and face him straight on, wanting him to see me when I punch him for the first time.

Raising my arm, my brothers close in as I punch him hard and fast. Sparky, Oak, Pope, and the others in the van don't move to stop me, knowing now of his treacherous betrayal, but all the others see it as their President being attacked. I wonder how long their loyalty will last once they find out what he's done? Not fucking long, I imagine.

I hold my arms up, showing them I'm finished.

"Tell them! Tell them how you used Alannah as bait. How you used her, your own blood!" I scream, the betrayal making my voice thick with emotion. "We never use women to do our work, never mind our blood."

The shock and gasps are audible.

"Nothing we did was good enough. The fuckers were one step ahead all the fuckin' time," he snarls, trying to defend himself to everyone.

"That's our world, not Alannah's. It's why we fucking fight every goddamn day," I remind him.

"If they'd been in the blast, we wouldn't be here now."

"No. If you hadn't put Barbie at risk, we wouldn't be here now," Sparky growls from behind me.

"I didn't want it to go down like this—it was a last resort. She'll be fine. They would've only taken her to get to us," he insists, trying to justify his actions.

"You saw what they did to Billy. They ain't gonna fuck about when it comes to her. Fuck, she killed two of their men. She's as good as dead because you... you couldn't get a grip on yourself," Oak stammers, barely containing his emotions.

"Your hatred for the Raging Riders has gone too far, and an innocent woman is paying the price," I tell him. I don't have the fight for him anymore. Hell, I can't even look at him.

"Makes me think of what you'd fuckin' do to one of us if you can to do this to your own niece," Pope spits, disgusted.

He has a point. A President holds all the respect in a club. No brother doubts him. No brother gives him anything less than their life and their loyalty, and what Michael's done has destroyed all of that.

One after the other, phones begin going off. I hear mine ring out, but I leave it in my pocket. Nothing's as important as this.

I grab Michael by his cut, ready to rip it from his back. No one is stopping me, staring at their phone screens in what can only be described as horror.

"Brother, you should take a look at this." Sparky tosses me his phone before he turns around and heaves on the grass.

Catching it in my free hand, I release Michael and hit play. Alannah and Hunter appear on the screen. She's bleeding from everywhere, and has her hands tied above her head. Hunter has his hand in her hair, yanking her head back. Motherfucker! I'm going to rip his fucking hands off. I barely hear his distorted voice, as I can't take my eyes away from my girl. When I see her spit at Hunter, covering him with her blood, I know she's trying to be brave. When I see her lose consciousness at the end, my heart sinks. We don't have much time before he beats her to the point of never waking up, just as they did to Billy.

I understand why Sparky's throwing up, because I could do exactly the same.

I shove the phone in Michael's face and hit play.

"Watch that and fucking tell me she's fine," I growl low and menacing. "You've done this."

His despair enrages me. I drop the phone and lay into him, feeling like I can't hit him hard enough. I want him to feel every bit of the pain Alannah has to be feeling.

Some fucking President we have. He curls up into a fucking ball to protect himself.

"Fucking take it, you piece of shit. Lana can't hide. Didn't watch long enough to see she's tied up with a goddamn rope around her fucking neck," I shout.

Sparky, Oak, Pope, Slade and a few others rush toward me. Lucky for Michael, they stop me because I can't stop myself. In fact, as soon as they let go of me, I run back to him and kick him repeatedly. Before I know it, I'm crashing to the ground, Sparky on top of me, pushing my head into the ground.

"We don't have time for this. Rein it in. We need to get her back, and we're not going anywhere fast here."

I can see Michael getting up from the ground, and all I want to do is beat him to death with my bare hands.

I continue to struggle under Sparky's hold.

"Brother, I'm fucking telling you, if you don't calm the fuck down she's gonna die. They'll kill her," he says slowly, making sure I take his words in. I do.

There's nothing I want more than to save her. Killing Michael will have to wait.

I stop resisting, and Sparky loosens his hold, only slightly.

"You good?" he asks.

Am I good? I'm far from fucking good, but I nod, and he raises himself off of me.

I roll onto my back and take his offered hand, steering clear of Michael.

"He's no brother of ours. Strip his cut and toss him in the van," I tell the group of brothers surrounding Michael.

"Castiel, don't do this to me," he begs.

"Don't fucking speak to me. The only way you're getting out of dying tonight is if you save Lana, and even then, I ain't fucking promising anything."

I head toward the van and turn. "We don't have much farther to go. We get there, we shoot our way in and take out every motherfucker in our path. I would say Hunter is mine, but I don't give a fuck who kills him, as long as he's put to ground."

Wisely, Michael is put in the other van for the rest of the drive. This is one big head fuck. I keep the images of Alannah beaten and bloody out of my head, as well as Michael's betrayal, and concentrate on how I'm going to make as many people as I can pay for hurting the only good thing in my life. If they plan on taking her from me, they better do it from my cold, dead fingers, because I'm not letting her go for nothing.

# 17

## Alannah

The warm, oblivious bliss soon ends when I feel myself moving about. Panicking, thinking I might slip off the crates, I open my eyes... well, one of them. The other one is swollen shut.

A Raging Rider I hadn't seen before is tugging at my jeans... oh God, no! I begin squirming away from him, but the farther back I move, the tighter the rope around my neck gets.

"Please, no," I cry out.

He looks up when he hears me and smiles. Nothing else, no reply. Just a smile.

I can't cope with the beatings, but they're a lot easier to endure than having this guy trying to rape me. I try screaming, but nothing comes out. My fear cripples me and diminishes my will to fight. I cry, tears mixing with blood burning my eyes. I squeeze them shut and pray. These men are nothing like the Lost Souls men. These men are rabid dogs, and the scariest part is there's no reasoning with them. I couldn't stay strong and show no weakness. I just cried.

The door opens, and feel a surge of relief. Hunter is no better, but in some strange way, I feel safer with him around —almost.

"You can have your fun later, Harry. I need her for now," he calls as he crosses the distance from the door to us. Harry sulks out of the room without a word.

"I was bored, so I thought I'd come and have a chat. You see, I have to get some things off my chest. As I said, I know all about you. I knew your daddy, know how close you were to Micky. You wanna know what happened to him?"

I really don't. I know enough, so I remain silent.

"I can show you if you'd like. I recorded it. No? Okay, fine. He was sent to deliver an envelope. I thought it was strange, but who am I to turn away an enemy? When he found out what he delivered, he kicked up a right fuckin' fuss. See, your precious club thinks he ratted them out. You should've seen his face when I read out loud what the message said. Your uncle betrayed him. The cunt had no clue what the envelope contained," he laughs.

I knew it. I knew Micky wasn't a rat. My uncle sent him in, knowing what would happen to him. I'm not given any time to dwell on it, as Hunter keeps his admissions going.

"I've got another surprise for you, bitch," he cackles, calling someone to come in.

I watch as a young, good-looking guy brings in a limping

girl, and my heart breaks again. It's Bonnie. Having more to fight for than just my life, I find my strength again. They must have taken her as she arrived at the cabin.

"She has nothing to do with this, you fucking animal. Let her go!"

She has a nasty bruise on her right cheek. Her lip is split like mine, and she's holding her ribs in pain. Seeing me hanging here, her eyes widen in horror.

Hunter laughs as he watches the two of us.

"She has everything to do with this, you stupid bitch. Who do you think led us to you? She's my daughter. She recognised you from the photos we have of you, and what would you know, you're at fuckin' college together. She's been feeding us your whereabouts for months."

"I don't believe you. She's nothing like you," I huff, not caring if my tears give my weaknesses away.

"I could've gotten to you anytime I fuckin' wanted. While I admit, I don't care for the cunt, she's still my daughter, and when your cunt of an uncle blew up my club, she caught the brush of it," he explains, pointing to Bonnie. "When we found her, she had a bag packed, and going through her phone, we found out she was on her way to you."

"She looks like she's been beaten, not blown up," I point out.

He turns his full attention to me. "Because she never learns her fuckin' place, just like you," he sneers, edging closer.

I cringe back as he brings his hand up again, but Bonnie's feral scream halts him.

"Please, Dad, don't hurt her," she cries.

"Shut up, bitch," the guy holding her arm growls at her.

Once she's quiet, Hunter hauls off and slaps me, causing her to scream out again. Hunter rounds on her and slaps her into silence before walking away, followed by the young lad.

When Bonnie hears the door slam shut, she's on her feet and limping quickly toward me.

"I promise you, I didn't give him anything, Alannah," she urges.

I have nothing left. With the men out of the room, I can relax, but that's when I truly feel the pain.

"Alannah, please, believe me," she prattles on.

"Run," I tell her weakly.

"I can't. They watch me as closely as they do you."

"Try. Please."

She drops to floor, and I wonder what she's doing until I feel my jeans being pulled back up my legs.

"I'm so sorry you're in this mess. You have to stop talking back to them or he'll kill you."

Her worry for me is painful to see.

"Then help me," I beg.

"I can't. The most I can do is stay close by and make a scene if they come back in," she whimpers, beginning to cry.

It's not fair of me to blame her. It seems she's as much a prisoner here as I am. I think back to all the times she returned to school in pain, and now I know why.

I flinch as she tries to wipe the blood off my face with her sleeve, so she leaves it be.

"Hey, Bonnie, get away from our guest," the young guy calls from the door.

She looks frantically between us. “I have to go. I’m so sorry… I’ll help if I can,” she whispers.

I’m then on my own again. Cas will come for me soon, I know it. I just have to keep myself alive until then.

# 18

## Cas

We're close. Another ten minutes and we'll be at the warehouse.

"We're going to fucking slaughter them all," Sparky promises.

Everyone mumbles in agreement, but I can't say a word. I roll my neck, trying to find some sort of release to all this building tension coursing through my body.

"I'm going to take them all out, pile them up in one fucking heap and blow them sky fucking high. There'll be body parts for miles around," he adds.

In a fucked-up way, it's soothing listening to the ways the cunts will be taken out.

I call Slade in the other van and tell him to signal to the others to drive in blind. They knew we'll be coming, but with our lights off, we can get a least a little closer before they see us coming.

The Raging Riders have their local law enforcement so deep in their pockets, they won't be a worry for us tonight.

"You'll make a fucking great President, brother," Sparky comments in my ear.

I huff. That's the last thing on my mind right now. Looking through the front of the van, I see the warehouse on the horizon.

"Right. Get ready, boys. When the van stops and the doors open, we start shooting like crazy motherfuckers. He'll have men on the doors, and I want them taken out before our feet hit the ground. Give our brothers a chance to make it off their bikes behind us."

No one can sit still, rocking and bouncing on the side shelves we use as seats.

"Cover each other and get in there fast. I need her back," I tell them, not caring that my anger is cracking in a begging urgency.

"She's coming home, Cas, you can fucking count on that," Sparky bellows.

She is coming home. I just pray she's alive when she does.

I quickly scan my brothers, knowing there's no other group of men I would feel safer with having my back, especially at times like this.

The first shot fired hits our van as we come to a screeching halt in front of the warehouse. Pope calls for us to get to the other end, which isn't an easy task. He slides the door open and fires shots at the three men at the door, who all go down before we're out of the van. All our brothers are behind us, jumping off their bikes and working fast to get a handle on their weapons.

A gun in each hand—one in the back of my jeans, and one in each pocket inside my cut—I'm more than prepared for this. Leading the men into the warehouse is eerie for the first ten seconds. It feels like I'm leading them like rabbits to their slaughter, and then shots are being fired from everywhere.

Fuck being rabbits. I shoot anywhere I see a body hiding or moving. I know every brother in my club so well, I don't need to worry about hitting the wrong side.

I was hoping for an open warehouse, maybe with a room or two off to the side, but this has corridors and rooms everywhere. The Lost Souls spread out. I make my way up one corridor, cautiously opening doors as I go. A Raging Rider fuck attacks me from behind a door. Momentarily stunned from the blow to the back of my head, I turn and swing my fist, connecting with his head. And like a sack of shit, he hits the floor, out cold. Shooting a man who's already unconscious isn't how I like to do shit, but he played a part in taking Alannah, and now he's paying the price. Squeezing the trigger, I shoot him once in the head and twice in his chest for good measure.

I leave the room and continue up the corridor, the sounds of gunfire echoing throughout the space.

As I near the end of the hallway, Sparky flies out of a room and crashes into the wall, his gun falling to the floor. As he bends down to pick it up, two rounds are fired into the wall where his head had just been seconds before. I run toward him, and we both shoot at the biggest fucking guy I've ever seen before.

"Thanks, boss," he pants, bending to his knees.

"No worries. Where the fuck is she?" I look in the room he'd just been thrown from.

"I don't know. There's more stairs over there." He points his gun in the direction he's speaking of.

"Come on, stick together. I'll go first," I murmur, passing him and heading for the stairs.

It's quiet up here. There are only four doors on this level. Everything screams of a trap.

"You take that side, I'll take this side. Be careful brother." I open the first door.

There's nothing but made-up beds on the floor. There's no one in them, and no places to hide. Closing the door, I move on to the next one.

Nothing again, but this room stinks of cigarette smoke and unwashed men, with makeshift chairs and tables set up in the small space.

"Cas," Sparky calls, drawing my name out warily.

I look down the hall and see him raise his gun.

# 19

## Alannah

I'm conscious when Hunter and the young lad return. It's hard not to hear the continuous gunshots being fired, telling me there are a lot of people fighting.

Hunter strolls toward me as if nothing's going on.

"Showtime, bitch." He smiles, exposing his yellow, broken teeth.

He nods for the lad to stand by the door. It's a prime position to take someone from behind as they come in.

The Lost Souls have arrived. Relief surges through me. Realising the lad's position will hurt someone I care about, my relief soon turns to dread.

Hunter takes his stance next to me and fists the rope and chain in his hand. I forgot what happens when I move, so when I twist away from him, the rope squeezes my neck again.

"Be a shame if you're dead before they make their entrance, don't you think, bitch?"

Fear for anyone being hurt, fear for not being saved, and fear for being saved but losing someone in the process finally makes me crack.

Hot, salty tears moisten the dried blood, and once again, my vision blurs red.

God knows how much time has passed, but as soon as the door bursts open, everything speeds up.

Not knowing who's on the other side, I cry out, protecting them the only way I can.

"Alannah?"

Sparky?

"There's a trap by the door."

Hunter pulls the rope, shutting me up. "Go. You know what to do," he tells the young lad. Running to other side of the room, he disappears through a different door I hadn't known was there.

Hunter remains at my side, waiting.

Yes, it's Sparky, calling for Cas. With no threat by the door, my relief returns. I have every faith they'll get me out of here.

Hearing boots pound against the floor as Cas races toward the open door, he barrels into the room, so closely followed by Sparky, he nearly crashes into his back when Cas abruptly stops at seeing me.

"Drop your guns, fuckers, or I'll let go of this bitch. The fall will snap her neck immediately," Hunter informs them.

The two men who would protect me until their dying breath stand motionless.

"How do we know you won't anyway?" Cas spits out.

I try blinking the blood and tears out of my eyes so I can see his face. If I'm going to die, I want his face to be the last one I see.

"All I want is Michael," Hunter tells them calmly.

After everything he had done to me, I believed him.

"What do you want with him?" Sparky questions.

"Old vendetta and payback. Now drop your fuckin' guns," he roars, and to show he means business, he pulls sharply on the rope, forcing it to tighten again around my throat.

Faster than Superman, they both throw their guns to the floor, shouting for him to stop.

Hunter keeps his word and loosens the rope. I gasp for air, my lungs screaming for it. I can't take any more. Where's my uncle? This will all stop when he gets here.

"Payback for what?"

I make eye contact with Cas, who's a deathly shade of pale, and hold his gaze. He's shaking. He told me once I would be the only one to take him out, and I see it in his eyes now. If I die here tonight, everything that makes him my Cas will die with me.

"As if you don't know."

"Apart from the fucking shit you've put my club through, it's nothing compared to what you've done to us."

"It has nothing to do with that, you dumb fuck," Hunter snaps back beside me.

"What, then?"

Sparky's keeping him talking, stalling for time, but none of that matters as I watch Cas trembling with anger and fear.

"I killed his fuckin' brother!"

Uncle Michael. He's here.

"Ah, nice of you to show your fuckin' face."

"You got me now, so let her go," Michael replies, getting closer.

"I've waited a fuckin' long time for this, Blake." I can hear the excitement for revenge in his voice.

"Well, I'm here, so come and fuckin' get me."

"I ain't stupid. Three on one isn't what I call fair. This is between me and you."

"Trust me, they ain't going to protect me. They're here for the girl only."

I tear my eyes away from Cas and look at my uncle. Why wouldn't they protect him? He briefly looks from Hunter to me, wearing an expression I've never seen on him before —guilt.

"Just to make sure, yeah?"

I'm so engrossed in trying to work out why Michael looks guilty, I never see Hunter's elbow coming, smashing into my face.

# 20

## Cas

I finally have her in my sights, and I can't do a fucking thing to help her. She looks worse off in person. Fear for her neck being snapped is the only thing keeping me rooted in place.

"Just to make sure, yeah?"

Hunter slams his elbow into her face. It could have been slow motion, or the fact I was watching them so intently, it made every movement look like a freeze frame image. Her head snaps back from the force of the impact, and doesn't come back up. The bastard knocked her out! The rope and chain he's holding goes slack as he releases his grip. His parting shot is to kick the crates out from under her before he makes a run at Michael.

The fucker made sure we were completely focused on Alannah, not believing we had no interest in helping Michael.

Whether he lives or dies at the hands of Hunter, I couldn't give a fuck less. All I care about is not allowing Hunter to live to see another sunrise.

Sparky flies past me, and every move, every battle cry, speeds up. Alannah's dangling from the above rafter, her body limp and lifeless. I snap into gear and run to her. It all happens in seconds. I pass Sparky and snatch her to my chest, lifting her above me to give slack to the rope choking the life out of her.

"Get her out of this," I order.

Sparky piles the crates on top of each other and climbs up so he can reach her restraints.

Cussing and calling out "Barbie," he has her released in less than a minute. I slide her down my torso and follow her to the ground.

Sparky untangles the rope around her neck and feels for a pulse. At his reassuring grin, I sigh out in relief. I hold her tighter in my arms, where she belongs.

"Wake up, Barbie!" Sparky pleads to her unconscious form.

I can see he's itching to slap her awake, but refrains because of her injuries.

"Let's get her the fuck out of here," he bites out, turning his glare on Michael and Hunter.

I look in their direction. Two grown men, their arms and legs kicking and swinging at each other. I honestly wouldn't be able to put money down on who will walk away from this. The raw, violent hunger coming from both of them is more than I've ever seen before. I've seen countless amounts of men fight, but nothing amounting to this level of pure hatred.

They both hit the floor and land near the guns Sparky and I had dropped. Obviously, moving on from hand-to-hand battle, they both lunge for the weapons. Hunter has an edge, in the lead, until Michael grabs hold of his ankle and pulls him back. Hunter's other foot slams into Michael's face and let's go, his nose busted for sure. Michael must have done some damage to Hunter, because he's not moving for the gun as fast as he should have been.

Michael gets himself together and raises himself up to his hands and knees. Catching up to Hunter, he knees him in the ribs and he stops immediately, giving Michael time to reach one of the guns and turn on his back. Hunter, getting over the last blow, charges toward him, and that's when Michael pulls the trigger—not once, not twice, but three times.

Hunter clutches at his stomach, wearing a startled expression. He truly thought he would walk away the victor tonight. Staggering around before slumping to the floor, I stare as he bleeds out, then draws his last breath. Michael relaxes his head back on the floor and drops the gun. Battered and out of breath, he throws his arm over his head and remains still, breathing heavily.

It would later occur to me that he didn't ask about Alannah, or even look her way.

Pope barrels through the door and scopes out the room. Seeing we're not in danger, his gaze lingers on Michael, who still hasn't moved. After a beat, his eyes lower to Alannah in my arms. Paling, he glares back at Michael and lowers his gun as he steps toward him.

Michael sees him coming and hoists himself to his knees. It turns my stomach that Pope is going to help him up. Him taking out the Raging Riders President doesn't mean shit to me, Sparky, or to any brother who loves Alannah.

I quickly look down to Alannah, who's still unconscious, then look back to Pope, his gun now aimed directly at Michael's head.

"What's going on?" Michael asks, his voice quivering with fear.

"Found me a real talkative Raging cunt. Tried to save his life by giving up some info on you," Pope replies neutrally.

"What are you talking about?" I ask.

"Found out what really happened to Micky," he chokes out, never looking away from Michael.

"And?" Sparky hisses.

"Turns out Micky was set up. He was meant to deliver a message, but he didn't know what it contained, not until that fuck read it to him," he spits at Hunter, dead on the floor.

Fuck. It never did add up. I hate myself, because a part of me believed he did rat on us. We buried him a traitor instead of a brother, and all this time it was Michael.

First, we find out he used Alannah as bait, and now we find out he sent a brother to his death, and not a quick one either.

I find myself nodding, and Pope nods back, understanding what I'm saying.

"Don't take me saving you from the club as kindness. It's 'cause I love my club that I'm doing it this way," he tells Michael. "Betrayal on this level would take the club years to get over. No trust within the club and we have nothing."

"Please, don't do this. Not having the club will be death enough for me," he begs.

"Not enough for me. Micky was our brother, and you killed him. No more."

Michael takes a few moments and pulls himself together. Straightening his shoulders and raising his head, he waits for the bullet. He's right. Without the club, he would be nothing, and that would the worst punishment a brother could endure. And Pope is right. Michael had gone too far, and he had to pay with his life.

"Hunter killed Michael, and I killed Hunter," Pope instructs us, putting pressure on the trigger.

Sparky and I both agree. Alannah's out cold, so she'll have no recollection of the lie.

Pope was also right when he said the club would take years to heal from this level of betrayal. It doesn't feel good knowing I'll have to lie to my brothers, to Kitty and to Alannah, but it has to be done.

"Get it over and done with, brother," Michael tells him.

"My traitorous brother, as you're about to walk through the valley of the shadow of death, the only evil you need fear is me, motherfucker."

This is where his nickname comes from. Every time he takes someone out, he turns biblical. He's never explained why he does it. The first time he did it, Michael asked him who the fuck he thought he was, the Pope? And from then on it stuck, and he's been called it ever since.

Michael holds his reserve and doesn't flinch once. Pope gets to the end of his sermon, and Michael knows he has seconds left of his life. He finally looks at Alannah, guilt crossing his face, and he briefly closes his eyes.

When he opens them, he faces Pope.

"I know you'll look after them, Castiel."

Pope pulls the trigger, and Michael lands on his back. One bullet between his eyes is all it took to take out the disgraced President of the Lost Souls MC.

Pope turns to us as he puts his gun in one of his pockets. "We clear what happened here?"

"Fuck yeah," we both reply at the same time.

"He was in a one-man war and used us as pawns. That's not a man we want at our backs."

He doesn't need to explain anything. Pope's not a man who says or does anything without facts and precision. It's also the most we've heard him say in one go.

We all grow quiet, taking in the scene before us, struggling to find words to say.

Alannah twitches in my arms, bringing me back to the present. Her eyelids flutter and her lips tremble. Pope removes his gun and shrugs out of his jacket, wrapping it around her.

"Get her out of here. I'll sort this shit out," he orders.

I lift her in my arms, careful not to press too hard, not wanting to hurt her further.

"I'll go first," Sparky offers, leaving in front of me.

Having my back, he peers out the door and checks the hall. Following him out when he gives the all clear, we make our way down two flights of stairs, continuously on our guard.

Thankfully, all the bodies we see on the floor are Raging Riders. Not one of our own as of yet.

The exit door is in our sights, and with no one around, we run the last distance together.

Outside are all our brothers—some wounded, some

completely fine. All have smiles on their faces and begin hollering when they see Alannah in my arms. Oak is the first one over.

"She okay?" he asks.

What he means is, is she alive?

"Yeah, but she needs the doc," I inform him, keeping a quick and steady stride to the van. We'd brought the club doc with us, hoping we wouldn't need him. He's a good friend of the club's, previously a medic in the army until his last tour in Afghanistan fucked with his head too much. He doesn't wear the cut, but he's just as important to us as a brother. The amount of questions we can avoid by using him is vital.

Everyone moves out of the way as I get closer. Sheets have been put down on the van floor, and with the help of Doc, I slide her onto them.

As much as I don't want to leave her, I have to check that everyone else is okay. She's in better hands than mine at the moment anyway.

Not moving far from the van, I look around, taking everything and everyone in.

"Is there a casualty count? Who's wounded?" I ask no one in particular.

Slade comes up beside me and begins firing off information.

"Three dead from the nomads and five wounded, including myself, but nothing too serious. Doc patched us up until we can get back to the clubhouse where he has more supplies."

Looking at his arm, I see the bandages wrapped around

his bicep. Wounded, I can deal with, but even one dead is one too many.

"I promise you all now, brothers, a night like this will never happen again. For those of you who can't ride, you'll travel in the vans. Whoever came in the vans and can ride, will ride your bikes back," I explain loud enough for everyone to hear.

"Let's get moving. We don't want to be here when the cops come and find their extra income riddled with bullets."

"Where's Michael?" I hear someone ask.

"Hunter shot him. He's dead," I declare. "Now, let's go."

# 21

## Cas

The ride home didn't feel as long as the ride there. Having Alannah back helped. It's very rare you see a brother break down and cry, but Sparky didn't try to hide it. Once Doc couldn't do any more for Alannah in the van, he made her as comfortable as he possibly could. I was on one side of her with Sparky on the other, each holding one of her hands. The last time she came around, Doc managed to get some pills down her throat to help with the pain.

Sparky held her hand in his, but it didn't stop the tears running down his cheeks. If I was insecure, I would've been jealous, but I know how close they've always been. I used to always think they would end up together because of their closeness. It was always his bike she would ride on the back of, and on party nights, he would spend his time with her instead of finding his dick a home for the night. I asked him once what he thought of her, and all he said was that she was his sister, and that was that.

"She's coming home, brother," I choke out.

"I swear to God, you better not let her out of your sight," he warns.

"I'm not fucking planning on it. She's going to be by my side morning, noon, and night," I promise him, and her.

An hour from home, I call the clubhouse and make sure they're ready for the extra visitors that will be bedding down for the night, insisting that my room is cleaned, and medical supplies are ready for when we arrive.

"We got a lot of shit to sort out, Cas," Sparky surmises, looking tired and rundown.

"We'll all get some rest and pick it up tomorrow." I'm not looking forward to any of it, though.

The prospect drives as close to the clubhouse as possible and opens our door.

Sparky and I lift Alannah out gently and carry her through the clubhouse bar and up to my room. The club girls gasp as we pass them, seeing the horrible extent of her injuries and imagining the hell she'd gone through. Satisfied with the fresh sheets and tidied room, we lay her on the bed and let Doc take a closer look at her.

~

Alannah wakes to Doc feeling her head. She barely has her eyes open before she's thrashing about, screaming the place down around us.

Doc jumps away and I take his place.

"Lana, it's me, Cas," I soothe. She's so terrified, she won't look at me.

Gripping her chin, she slowly tries to open her eyes, as one is swollen shut, still whimpering.

"You're safe. I got you," I tell her quietly.

She takes in her surroundings before looking above her head, and then down to her arms, gripping my tee. As if she doesn't believe she's free, she checks above her head again.

"It's okay. You're home, you're with me, and you're safe," I repeat.

I feel her relax, but her face scrunches up in pain.

"I hurt so bad," she cries.

"I know you do, baby. Doc was checking you over to see if you need to go to the hospital."

She loosens her grip and drops her arms to the bed.

"Let him check you over. I promise you, he won't hurt you."

I go to move so Doc can carry on with his assessment, but she snatches my hand in hers. She doesn't have to ask. I move up the bed to give Doc the room he needs and keep her hand in mine.

Everywhere Doc touches her, she cries out. I didn't shed one tear when I first saw her tied up. I didn't shed a tear when I saw how bad she was in the van. But hearing her in pain, knowing there's not a fucking thing I can do about it, the tears start to come. Just like Sparky, I don't try to hide them or wipe them away.

"Nothing's broken. She's very badly bruised, and the cuts on her head and face aren't deep enough to require stitches. Given what she went through, she could've been a lot worse," he concludes, gathering up the leftover medical supplies. "Give her these, one every four hours, and these if she needs them in between. I gotta go see the walking wounded out there." He hands me two different bottles of pills.

"Let her rest. One of the best remedies for the human body is rest," he adds before walking out and down the hall.

Doc had only given her a dose of pain relief ten minutes ago, so I keep my eye on the clock and set my phone alarm for four hours' time.

I doubt she'll wake in the next couple hours, and as much as I don't want to leave her, I know she's safe enough here for me to take the quickest shower of my life to wash away her blood and the other's I feel dried onto me.

First, I find one of the club girls and ask her to fetch me a bowl of soapy warm water and clean cloths, and have them ready on the bar in ten minutes. It's going to be bad enough for Alannah to see her injuries; she doesn't need to see the blood encrusted on her as well.

Fresh out of the shower and in clean sweats and a long-sleeved tee, I head directly for the bar. I have my back to everyone as I try to gather the soapy water, cloths, and a shot of whiskey that's pushed on me. I don't want to lose myself in alcohol just yet, but man, I need at least a shot of something hard.

The sound of applauding from behind me increases and gets louder. I turn to see what the hell is kicking off now, and

I'm dumbstruck when I see each and every brother facing me. What the fuck?

I'm about to ask when Oak comes and stands next to me. Slinging his arm around my shoulders, cheers with everyone else.

"Brothers, please, some quiet!" he yells. After a minute, he has their silence and attention.

"Not only were we betrayed by a man who was our brother, but a brother who was our President," he begins, pausing to take another swig from his bottle. "He not only led us to believe one of our own had turned against us, but he used a woman for his own needs. We buried Micky with disrespect when all along he deserved retribution! You've all seen what happened to Alannah, and we lost three of our brothers tonight as well. Billy, who Michael sent to his death knowing—no, hoping it would end the way it did, all because he lost his sense of brotherhood and of family."

Everyone whispers or nods their agreement. "Michael got greedy, and we ain't greedy men. All we want is a few dollars in our pocket, a drink in our hand, a woman in our bed, and the road beneath our bikes."

Everyone erupts into agreement, throwing "fuck yeahs" and "hell yeahs" about.

"For a while now, Castiel Jackson here has proven he can guide and lead us. I trust him with my life, and I trust him with all yours too. Is there a brother here against Cas becoming President of our mighty fine fuckin' club?" he bellows.

Nobody disagrees. I look around at all my brothers, not a single one opposing me taking the position.

Shit. The last time I felt like this, I'd been made Vice President. They trust me not only with their lives, but with their families and their club. I can't find any words to say, apart from to stand rooted in place with my mouth hanging open— not very Presidential-like at all.

I recognise Sparky handing Oak my cut. Having been wiped clean of blood, he takes it and faces me, holding it out for me to slip into.

Once it's in place, I look down at the new patch that's replaced my VP one, now reading "President."

Oak raises my arm in the air with his and shouts out, "Our President!"

That's it. The whole place practically shakes from every brother who can move, man hugging each other, jumping, and cheering at the top of their lungs.

I'm passed around the room, being congratulated, told how well I executed tonight's rescue plan, how much I deserve the position, and how I have their loyalty.

"Told you you'd make a fucking great President," Sparky says, slapping me on the back.

"Fuck off. You didn't know I would be President then," I laugh, remembering when he said it in the van.

"I fucking did. Once you stripped Michael's cut, I knew it would be you who took over."

Hearing the sincerity in his words, I almost choke up when I say, "Thanks, brother."

"This calls for a celebration," someone shouts from somewhere in the crowded bar.

I stand near the bar and raise my hand for them to be quiet.

"I ain't gonna get all soft on you fuckers, but I just want to say thanks. Not just for having faith in me and making me your President, but for tonight. You're what brotherhood is about. We all had each other's backs. We lost four members, but we'll never forget them. And along with Micky, we'll show them the respect and love in a send-off they'd be proud of." Those who have a drink, which is most of them, raises their glasses and bottles in the air. "The shit with the Raging Riders is over, and as your President, I swear to you we'll bring this club back to its former glory."

It takes a full minute for them to quiet down again so I can continue.

"I'll celebrate when my old lady is here to celebrate with me, but tonight, brothers, drink and party without me, you deserve it. If it weren't for you fuckers, I wouldn't have been able to bring her home."

I raise the glass of whiskey I'd managed to keep hold of in the air.

"To the Lost Souls!" I yell, necking my shot of whiskey.

While the crowd continues to celebrate, I escape before they grow more boisterous, grabbing hold of the soapy water —which is surprisingly still warm—and slip away, back to Alannah.

I close the door quietly behind me and lock it. Alannah hasn't moved from when I left for a shower. I didn't intend to be so long, but fucking hell, I never expected what just happened. Sure, if I had the time to think about it, I might've saw it coming, but this changes everything. I still answer to my brothers, but I never needed their permission for nothing. No doubt about it, Alannah is coming home to the club, where she should have been from the start. Sitting on the edge of the bed, I set about cleaning the blood off her face, careful not to touch the butterfly stitches she has in place.

Hunter should be glad he's dead, and hopefully burning in hell, because it looks like her face is covered in all sorts of different colour bruises, and I want to hang him by his arms and beat the shit out of him myself.

Satisfied, I remove as much of the blood as I possibly can, clear away the red-stained bowl of water, and throw the blood-soaked cloths away. She's positioned dead center in my bed. I don't want to accidently hurt her by laying with her, so leaving the room for less than a minute, I find a chair and put it as close to the bed as possible.

I meant what I said earlier. Until she's well enough not to leave my side, I'm not going to leave hers.

I flip off the overhead light and turn the small lamp on. Taking my seat in the chair, I watch her, sometimes peacefully, sometimes whining in her sleep. I wipe away more tears that spring from my eyes, knowing how lucky I am to have her back. Not only from the Raging Riders, but back in my life. It was a long year waiting for her, but we got there, and she's mine—definitely mine.

After a couple of hours, there's a knock on the door. I jump up and quickly answer it before they wake my girl up.

It's Pope.

"Can't this wait until morning?" I ask him, walking into the hall and pulling the door closed behind me.

"Thought you'd like to know, I burnt them all to a crisp. They'll be lucky if they can identify any of them. I moved

Michael's body, burnt it, and buried it in an unmarked grave. No comebacks on us," he informs me through a yawn.

"Good. Get some sleep. You look like shit," I say through my own yawn.

He turns to leave, but quickly backtracks.

"How is she?"

"She's going to be all right." I smile.

He nods and heads for his own room down the hall.

I slump into the chair again and close my eyes. I was fooling myself to think I could stay awake. I'm exhausted, physically and mentally.

Tomorrow's a new day, and I need to be ready for it.

# 22

## Alannah

Pain wakes me. I open my eyes—one of them, anyway—hoping to see Cas, but all I see is the soft glow of light and darkness behind it. Was coming home a figment of my imagination? Had I imagined being saved to take me away from the pain of Hunter?

The thought of my imagination playing tricks on me petrifies me. I hear movement and can't help screaming. I can't take anymore.

"No, please... no more," I beg as I feel hands on me.

"It's me, babe, Cas."

I barely hear him through my sobbing. My body shudders, and even knowing I'm in Cas's arms can't stop it. I'm safe, yet I don't feel free.

"I got you, babe," he repeats again and again, until my sobs ebb away, and my body melts into his.

His phone shrills from his bedside table, causing me to jump out of my skin.

"It's okay, it's just my alarm. It's time for you to take your meds," he coos, leaning back on the pillows.

He reaches for the glass of water and a bottle of pills, which I take without hesitation.

"No one is ever going to touch you ever again, I fucking promise you," he swears.

I want to reach out and stroke his cheek, but my arm aches from my shoulder to my hand.

"They were... animals," I say shakily.

I'm sure there's a harsher word or phrase I could use to describe them, but I can't think of one right now. Then it dawns on me. I don't remember coming home.

"How did we get out?"

His face transforms into something I don't want to understand.

"Maybe you should get some rest first. We've got plenty of time for talking when you're better." He stares at my hand, the one he's holding, stroking it lightly.

Now I really want to know.

"Tell me."

He sighs heavily and looks at me.

"What do you remember last?"

I think back. It's hazy, but I remember Uncle Michael, and how guilty he looked, then nothing.

"Hunter was next to me, and then I woke up here," I tell him.

"Maybe it's better if you don't know..."

"Please. I want to know."

"All Hunter wanted was Michael. He wanted to fight him one-on-one, without me or Sparky jumping in. So he knocked you out, kicked the crates out from under you, and left you to hang," he says in a rush.

I gasp, and instinctively grab my throat. It feels sore when I swallow, but on the outside, I can't feel anything. God knows how long I was tied there. I was terrified Hunter or one of his men would watch me hang, and when it happened, I just wasn't conscious to see it myself. I gasp for breath, not only because of what happened to me, but because I could be dead now, and Cas would have seen me die, leaving him forever.

"I'm... so... sorry," I pant.

"Calm down, Lana. Breathe, and then tell me what the fuck you got to be sorry about," he says, rubbing at my shoulders. That makes it worse, and I flinch away from him. Taking it the wrong way, he backs off.

"Don't go. It just hurt when you did that," I insist, my breathing returning to normal.

"Shit, I didn't think... Sorry," he mumbles, moving closer. "Now tell me what you got to be sorry for?"

"Because you had to see me like that. You must have thought I was dead."

"Fuck, Lana, that shit wasn't your fault. We had you out of that thing in seconds. I wasn't letting you leave me."

His tone is ferocious, causing tears to fall down my cheeks. He really does love me.

"What happened after?"

I'd stayed strong throughout my ordeal, and for some reason, I needed to know how it ended.

"Hunter and Michael got into it. I missed most of the fight, as I was concentrating on getting you free. By the time we knew you were alive, the fight was pretty much over."

My heart's thumping. Why did he stop? What isn't he telling me?

"Who won? How's my uncle?" I question.

"No one won. They're both dead," he says matter-of-factly, not sugar coating it either. Not that I gave a fuck about Hunter, but Michael?

Although, how does both of them being dead work? He sees my confusion and says, "A lot's happened in the last day, babe. I'm not going to hide anything from you, because I don't want to have secrets between us. Being my old lady just bumped you up to the MC Queen. I'm going to need you by my side like never before, and to understand what's going on, you need to know the truth. It's going to hurt you, and you're not going to be able to talk about it to anyone but me..." He pauses. I wait for him to speak again, but he's taking his time.

"Just spit it out, Cas."

He scrubs his face with his hand and forces himself to look at me.

"Pope killed Michael after Michael killed Hunter."

Pope killed Michael? No, this couldn't be true. Pope would never do that.

"Why?" I'm not going to break down yet. I have to remain as calm as I can until I know all the facts.

"Your uncle, my brother, deserved to die. You remember being adamant Micky wasn't a rat?"

As soon as he says it, I remember Hunter telling me the truth about Micky.

"Well, you were right. Michael led him into a trap."

"I know. Hunter told me about that. I knew Micky wouldn't do that. I just don't understand why Michael would do that to him," I squeak out.

"That's not all, babe. You wondered why he made you leave the club? It was because he'd planned it that way. Keeping me away from you, you out in the middle of nowhere… he used you as bait," he mutters, whispering the last five words.

"But he made Billy stay with me. Why would he do that if he wasn't looking out for me?"

As soon as I say his name, everything that happened at the cabin comes back to me.

"Oh God. Where's Billy? Is he okay? Is he here?" I shriek.

"Lana, Billy died just after we turned up at the cabin."

No words, just pain.

It's too much to comprehend. My uncle using me, using Micky, and as good as killing Billy himself. If Michael hoped I'd be taken, he'd have known a prospect would've fought to the end to protect me, all the time knowing he never would've stood a chance against the Raging Riders on his own.

My fury overtakes the pain and grief taking root inside of me. All Billy wanted was to be a part of the club, and he died a fucking puppet.

Images of him still trying to protect me from Biker Two spring to mind. Being thrown against the wall and landing in a puddle of blood on the floor.

I feel sick. I close my eyes to the extreme guilt sweeping over me.

"Did you see what they did to him?" he asks.

I open my eyes, not particularly wanting to relive it again, but wanting Cas and everyone to know how hard Billy fought to try and save me. He deserved that.

I recount everything from the start, when I heard the van doors slamming shut.

"I tried to save him. He told me to shoot them, but Hunter wouldn't stop kicking him. You should've seen the blood, Cas... he was in so much pain. I threw down the gun, hoping he would leave Billy alone. One of the guys came to get me, and Billy still tried to defend me, but he got another beating. I was taken into a van, and all I could see was Hunter stomping on him. He told me to hide at first. Maybe if I had, he would still be alive?" I sob, becoming more hysterical as I explain.

Cas pulls me into arms. I'm crying so hard, I don't register the pain. Physical pain would be better than this.

"Even if you hid, they would've pulled apart the cabin to find you, and I'm sorry to say, but Billy was always going to die."

I pull back in shock, staring at him, waiting for him to explain what he means.

"Using you as bait, Michael signed Billy's death certificate the day he put him at the cabin with you. When we arrived, he was still trying to save you. He was dragging himself from the house to his truck. He wasn't just your friend, Lana. You were his, and he wasn't alone when he passed. His brothers were with him. After everything he went through, he died smiling because I made him a full member."

"You did?" I can't stop the small smile that crosses my lips. Billy's smile would've been bright knowing he made it into the club.

"I did. Poor fucker deserved it. I knew if he didn't fight

back hard, they would've simply shot him to get to you. He tried to take them all on to save you, knowing he couldn't win, but he still tried. That's loyalty, and that's why I made him a brother."

I want to thank him. I want to make everything right, but the grief consumes me, the tears never stopping until Cas lays me back on the pillow and holds me, letting me get it all out.

~

Over the next two days, I slept on and off, only leaving the bed to go to the bathroom. I welcomed sleep, it took the pain away, and everything that caused it in the first place. I cried for Micky and everything he went through. I cried for Billy and the life he would never know as a Lost Soul. I didn't cry for my uncle, I cried because of what he'd done. Cas told me three brothers had died the night they rescued me, and I cried for them and for their families. Cas never left my side. Each time I woke, screaming from my nightmares, he would be right there, holding me, promising me I was safe. And then when I cried, it hurt, knowing just how much he loved me.

Waking up today, I feel a lot better, not as tired and achy. Cas is asleep beside me, and I don't want to wake him. After about five minutes, I manage to get out of bed on my own, and gingerly make my way to his bathroom. That's when I see my reflection for the first time in his mirror.

I look ghastly. On closer inspection, I can't make out one single bruise, as they blend in a mix of black, purple, green, and yellow shades of awful. Parts of my hair are matted to my scalp from the dried blood, and God, do I stink. How the hell has Cas not thrown me into a bath already? I set about turning the shower on and brush my teeth until the water's warm enough to step into.

Just having clean teeth makes me feel a lot better. When Cas first undressed me out of my bloodstained clothes, it hurt to put a tee over my head, so I've been in nothing but my bra and his sweats.

I slip out of both and step under the warm spray of water. Working as quickly as I can, I wash my hair and body—once, twice, and on the third time, I lather my body in soap until I feel I've washed away that awful night. This being the longest I've stood up in the last few days, rounds of dizziness catch me off-guard a couple of times. Grabbing onto the railing, I see the bruises on my wrists, instantly remembering being tied up, the warehouse, Hunter, and the other dirty animals who took me. My legs give out and I slide to the basin floor, gasping for breath as I let the water wash over me. I know I'm safe, I'm home, and there's a bunch of men out in the bar area who would throw down their life for me if anyone dared to come in here, yet I can't shake the fear that racks my body into submission.

"Lana?"

I hear the bathroom door open, and Cas pulls the shower curtain away. He looks like an angel bearing down on me. Stepping into the shower, he turns it off and lifts me out. Wrapping me in towels, he carries me back to bed.

"What were you thinking? Why didn't you wake me up?" he demands, drying me with one of the towels.

"I didn't want to wake you. You're so tired already, and I

thought I was okay, then I saw these and freaked out," I groan, holding my bruised wrists out.

"I don't care how tired I am, it's still nothing compared to what you're fucking going through. Next time, wake me up," he bickers.

I nod and wipe away my tears.

"Listen, I can't prolong it anymore. I have to go to church today."

My eyes dart to his. It's true, he hasn't left my side. I'd forgotten there would be a lot to sort out. For one, they would need to elect a new President to take my uncle's place.

I'm about to ask a million questions, when there's a soft knock on the door.

"It's open," Cas calls out as he buttoned his jeans and slides into his cut.

The door opens, and Sparky enters. When he sees me sitting up, his face breaks out into a gorgeous grin. I pull the sheet up around me and smile back.

"Barbie, you're finally awake... and clean," he laughs warily, still looking at me.

"Yeah, I'm okay, so you can stop looking at me like that," I tell him.

He crosses the room and wraps his arms around me, hard enough to show me how much he cares, but gentle enough to not hurt me.

"So fucking happy you're all right, Barbs," he whispers into my neck.

"Me too."

He releases me when Cas purposely clears his throat.

"Don't be getting jealous, Pres. My love for your girl is one hundred percent platonic," he teases.

Pres? Cas never told me. I scan his cut and see the newly sewn patch on the left side of his chest.

My mouth falls to the floor, and they both chuckle. Cas leans on the bed and kisses into my mouth because I have yet to close it.

"Told you, you'd become the MC Queen," he chuckles again.

"Congratulations," I grin. "In that case, your Queen would like to go see the minions while you do business," I laugh. Then, on a more serious note, I say, "I don't want to stay here on my own."

He frowns, but sets about finding me some clothes. He turns to Sparky, who gets the message, and leaves the room as my man helps me into his hoodie and clean sweats.

"You remember when I told you, you weren't my Vice President, just my Cas?"

He nods, staring at me intently as he pulls the hoodie carefully over my head.

"Well, now you're the President, but to me, you're still just my Cas."

"I'm anything you want me to be, babe," he promises. "Let's go."

He goes to help me walk, but as the President's old lady, I'd now have to be seen as strong, and as much as I want to be close to him all the time, I have to do this myself. I take his hand, excited to be able to be seen together by anyone, and leave his room for the first time in days.

"Oh, by the way, if you expect me to stay in your room,

you're buying a new bed. God knows who's been in it before," I inform him before we get to the top of the stairs.

"Yeah. So this is what it feels like to have an old lady, huh? Bossing me around already," he smirks, looking down at me.

I grin back. "Someone's got to. Now that you're the boss, I wouldn't want your ego getting too big."

He carries on laughing until we get to the bottom of the stairs, where I'm welcomed with hoots and hollers. Oak comes over first, and I sink into his embrace.

"It's fuckin' good to see you up and about, darlin'."

"It feels good."

"Come on, let's get you a chair. You should still be resting," he murmurs, tugging me to one of the sofas.

He gives me a quick kiss on the cheek before moving away. It seems a line has formed of brothers, and if I'm seeing correctly, some of the club whores too.

As they ask how I am, and if there's anything they can do for me, I thanked them for everything they did. Cas and Sparky may have set me free, but they wouldn't have been able to do it without these men here.

Slade is the last brother to hug me before Cas calls church and the bar empties, but he jogs over and makes sure I'm okay before he joins them.

"Never seen anything like it, babe. I should get you a crown," he chuckles.

"Don't you dare. Although, some pretty jewels wouldn't be rejected," I laugh. "Now go on. Go do President things."

He kisses me softly and leaves, throwing his phone in the box before closing the door behind him.

I'm feeling tired now I'm on my own. Ricky and Jack, the

two prospects, are working behind the bar, a few girls waiting around for them to finish. If you take away the layers and layers of make-up, and the bags under their eyes, they're actually quite pretty, even Danni. Watching her clip-clop toward me in her ridiculously high heels, I wish I would've pretended to be asleep.

"Hey, honey," she says in her stupid high voice.

Honey? Oh God, shoot me now.

I keep silent, waiting for her to say what she came to say.

"Is there anything I can get you?"

Wow, I wasn't expecting that.

"A bottle of water would be good, thanks."

She half-turns, then stops and faces me.

"I also wanted to tell you, I'm sorry. I didn't know what was happening with you and Cas last year. And at the cabin, your uncle told me Cas had asked for me. I want you to know you don't have to worry about me making a play for your man. And for what it's worth, he wouldn't come near me anyway. If you saw what he was like when you were taken, well... He loves you, girl, and no one's coming between that."

She takes my breath away. Does she expect me to believe her? I don't need her to tell me Cas loves me. I know it, but I also know these girls don't care who their fuck has at home, just as long as they get their night of attention and a few dollars thrown at them every now and then.

"You don't believe me, I can see it in your eyes. It's true. I may do a lot of things to make people think I'm a slut, but I don't play for taken men."

She sounds genuine enough. I suppose time will tell if she's telling the truth.

"Thanks, I appreciate you telling me that. But I'm not worried. You see, I'm not like some of the other old ladies. I'm not stopping Cas from touching any of you girls, but he sure fucking knows the consequences if he does, and he knows it won't be fucking pretty. The same goes for whoever he goes with."

She swallows hard and nods.

"I'll take that bottle of water now," I remind her.

She flitters back to the bar, and I take in every inch of the room. Nothing has changed since I left, and I'm happy to be back.

# 23

## Cas

I feel the power surge through me as I bring down the gavel on the old wooden table for the first time as President.

"Sorry I haven't called this meeting sooner, boys, but I wanted to make sure Lana was okay, and we all needed the downtime after all the shit we've been through lately," I tell them all.

"I swore the club would change, but first we all need to be clear on what happened in order for us to move on. So, if anyone has anything on their mind, bring it to the table now."

"I've been out my nut on whiskey since we got back, and only just putting everything together. What happened to Michael's body?" Oak asks, everyone looking at each other.

They know he's dead, but nothing else.

"To show him the disrespect he showed us, I burnt his

body on top of Hunter's and the rest of his enemies," Pope replies from the other end of the table.

I don't want to lie to my brothers, nor does he or Sparky, but we know it's for the best, and once this is finished with, we'll bury it, along with all traces of Michael.

"It's what he fuckin' deserved," Oak mumbles.

"What about Hunter's daughter? She wasn't there, which means she's still out there somewhere. Have you spoken to Alannah about her yet? Does she know who she really is?" Slade inquires.

"No, it's been hard enough telling her about Michael and Billy. Do we really need to worry about one woman? She hasn't got the club behind her now," I say.

"Alannah might know something about her. We shouldn't dismiss her so soon, Cas. She might go one-woman crazy on us with vengeance for killing her father," Slade argues.

He has a point. I was expecting us to put the club to rights and move on. I don't want anything hanging over us.

"Okay, check her out. Look into her whereabouts, where she may be hiding, and we'll go from there. I don't want Alannah to know nothing about it, though. She doesn't need this shit on top of everything else right now."

He nods and sits back in his chair.

"With me becoming President, my old patch needs to be put on a cut."

I pull my old VP patch out of my pocket and slam it on the table in front of Sparky.

"Y–You're making me Vice President?" he stutters in disbelief.

"Yes, and Slade will become our new Road Chief."

Slade's eyes shoot to mine and he nods. It's about time he wore the patch. He's been here for years, and he'll do just as good a job as Sparky has.

"Okay, moving on. We need to arrange four fucking funerals. I want every brother from all chapters here paying their respects. As you all know, I made Billy a full member, and we'll show him the same respect, because he deserves it."

'Ayes' are called out around the table, and fists are banged against the tabletop to show their agreement.

"Between you all, get in contact with everyone you can and let them know next Monday, they're to be here to say goodbye. Until then, we need to prepare ourselves. We're going to need to make a lot of room to house everyone. It'll be tight, but it can and will be done."

"I'll get the girls on it," Sparky advises.

"Good. Make sure they have anything they need. Next, I want to bring the prospects to the table. How do you feel about them making the cut? Ricky has been here just over a year, and Jack eight months. They've proven they have what it takes to deal with shit, and from what I've heard, they fought as hard as we did."

"Sparky?"

"Yeah." One vote.

"Slade?"

"Hell yeah." Two votes.

"Oak?"

"They'll make fine brothers, so yeah." Three votes.

"Pope?"

"From what I saw, I'd trust them with my life as much as I do you. I vote yes."

Four votes.

I continue around the table, and no one's against it.

"Call them both in, Pope."

I stand and pull the cuts with their new patches out from under the table. I've had a lot of time to think while I've been with Alannah. I had my suspicions the table wouldn't vote against them, so I had their cuts they would wear until the day they died made.

They both come in, wondering what the hell is going on. Pope takes his seat, and they remain standing by the door, looking nervous.

"Jack, Ricky, you've been here a while now, and we all agree you've both proven yourselves to us and to our club. No longer will you be referred to as prospects, but as brothers."

As the President of their MC, I round the table with their cuts and hold them up for them to wear. One by one, they put their arms through and are welcomed to the brotherhood by all.

"We're going to need more chairs," Sparky laughs.

"Fuck that. We're going to need more prospects. I ain't serving myself at the bar," Oak mumbles as everyone breaks out into laughter.

A weight has been lifted off the club, we can all feel it. Hopefully, the lack of chairs around the table and recruiting more prospects will be as bad as it gets from now on.

"Is there anything else anyone wants to bring to the table?" I asked.

"Yeah. When are we gonna fucking celebrate you becoming President?" Sparky hollers.

"With the Raging Riders gone, we'll get the funerals out of

the way, and then we'll celebrate. A new start for us all." I bring the gavel down, ending the meeting.

Everyone begins to leave, apart from Sparky and myself. Once we're alone, the fucker goes all soft on me.

"Thanks, Cas. I won't let you down, brother."

"I know you won't. You haven't so far."

"Damn straight I haven't, and never will." He smirks.

"Alannah told me before that you've met this Bonnie friend of hers. Do you think we could have a problem with her in the future?"

"I only met her a few times, and every time I spoke to her, she would clam up and fuck off. I would say unless she's a great fucking actress, I'd be surprised if she said boo to a ghost."

That makes me feel a little better. Sparky has a sense for people. It would be stupid of me to completely ignore her, but for now, I can put her to the back of my mind.

"Come on. You might not want to celebrate your new position, but I fucking do." Slapping his hand on the table, he stands and turns to leave.

"All right. I want to see how Lana is anyway."

Leaving the room, Sparky makes his way to the bar, while I lean against the door after I close it. Alannah is still on the sofa, talking to one of the club girls, which surprises me. Thank God it's not Danni. I damn sure don't fancy picking up clumps of hair off the floor.

Her bruises don't faze me at all. She's still as beautiful to me as she was before she was taken. Although, it does remind me of how easily I could have lost her. The bruises will heal, and she'll be back to her jaw-dropping self in no time. All that worries me is the psychological damage she may have. She's always been strong, but what she went through is going to leave its mark on her. I just hope she can find a way to work through it when the time comes.

As if she feels me watching her, she looks straight at me and smiles, visibly relaxing.

Yeah, her smile tells me she'll be just fine—in time.

When I walk over, the club girl smiles and disappears. Taking her place, I put my arm around my girl, careful not to hurt her. She leans in close and runs her finger along my "President" patch.

"Did it feel good being President in there?" she asks.

"Not as good as it feels being inside you," I whisper in her ear.

Her giggle warms me. Yeah, I know she'll be okay.

"Be serious," she warns.

"It felt fucking great. Sorted through a lot of shit, rearranged the men a little, and made plans for the funerals. They're next Monday."

She stiffens beside me, and tries to control her breathing.

"Billy should have a cut," she murmurs, and then adds, "I'd like to stitch his patch on."

I'd already had a cut made for him and his patch sewn on, but she doesn't know that. I make a mental note to have one of the girls remove it so Alannah can do it herself. She blames Michael a whole lot for Billy, but she also blames herself. If this is what she wants to do for him, I'll make it happen.

"Sure. You feeling okay? You want me to take you back to my room?" I ask.

"No. They need their President here with them. I told you, I can share you with the club, but no one else."

I feel on top of the fucking world right now. All every brother wants is his old lady to love him and to love the club just as much, and to understand how the club works. I've hit the fucking jackpot with Alannah Blake. Not only does she love me, but she loved the club long before I turned up.

"I love you so fucking much, babe," I tell her, moving so I can see her face.

"I love you too."

I want to smash my lips against hers, but before I can, hers are on mine. In front of everyone, she stakes her claim on me, just like I always hoped she would.

# 24

## Alannah

It's been a week since the club changed forever, and today we say goodbye to our friends and family. I still look horrendous, but I'm feeling a hell of a lot better than I did a few days ago. I've stayed at the clubhouse since the attack, not even leaving the compound. When Cas suggested going back to the cabin to pick up some things I might like, I freaked. I can't face going there yet. Last time I was there, Billy was alive, I knew nothing of my uncle's betrayal, and I was happy being in love with Cas. All that has changed now. The thought of going back there and seeing where Billy was murdered makes me feel sick.

Cas had someone go out and buy a new mattress and bedding for his room. I wasn't sure he would follow through, but he did.

The clubhouse has been welcoming members from all over the last few days, so there's been a lot of drinking and commiserating going on. I've shown my face and thanked everyone who came to save me. I know I didn't have to, but I wanted to.

Yesterday, I visited my Aunt Kitty. She had her friends around her, cooking for her and making sure she ate and bathed, but she wasn't there, not emotionally. Cas told me he explained everything to her, but she wasn't believing any of it. She wouldn't talk to me or look at me. She blamed me for his death, and apparently, it was all my fault. I should've been upset, but I wasn't. I knew how much she loved Michael, and if blaming me was what she needed to get through her grief, then she can blame me all she likes.

I'd heard she wasn't coming to the funerals today. I didn't want to try and make her.

My relationship with Cas has grown stronger every day. When he's not busy with the club, he's with me. Covered in bruises still, I stare in the mirror and wonder what to do with myself. Do I blacken my eyes to match my dress? If I do, it would only run when I cried later, and I'm positive I will cry. Opting for foundation and concealer only, I cover my bruises until I can hardly see the discolouring on my face. Tying my hair into a simple ponytail, I slide a black flower behind my ear and give myself a final once-over.

I jump up when Cas comes in. The guilt I feel every time I do it, through no fault of his own, tears at me.

He's wearing his black jeans, a long-sleeved black tee with his cut over it, and his hair is pulled back. I feel bad for thinking how hot he looks today of all days.

"Ready, babe? Everyone's waiting." He holds his hand out for me.

"Do I look okay?" I ask. I'm not fishing for compliments. I want to make sure I look good at Cas's side. Even though today is for mourning, I still have to maintain my position as the President's old lady, and I want to look the part.

"Babe, you look more than okay."

When we exit the clubhouse, Cas leads me past the many, many bikes, and to one of the two cars the old ladies are riding in behind the hearses.

Everyone, apart from Cas, are on their bikes. He makes sure I'm seated and closes the door. I watch through the window as he walks to his bike and climbs on, wrapping his bandana around his face. He revs up his bike, and in turn, so does everyone else, the noise thunderous. He rides out first, followed by everyone in our chapter. The hearses begin moving, then us, and from what I can see, there must be well over a hundred bikes as far as the eye can see behind us.

I tuned out most of the service. For a bunch of bikers, they made today beautiful. Five black coffins hovered above five empty graves side by side, a sheet with the Lost Souls emblem covering each coffin top. Brothers from far and wide stood with their arms crossing their chests in respect, while the old ladies sat on folding chairs in center position. I made the mistake of sitting on the end, facing Billy's coffin.

I asked Slade to double check he had no family. Of course, everyone was mourning him today, but there's nothing like having your blood there to say goodbye. He hadn't been able to find anyone, so I made it my mission to make sure if he was looking down on us, he would know how much I miss him and how much he meant to me.

I stare at his coffin, then to the sky. The sun is partly covered with clouds, and a flock of birds' circle above us.

"If you're there, Billy, please believe how sorry I am. I should have shot them. I wish you were still here to see what your life would've been like as a brother. All you saw was the bad. I'm sorry I took that away from you. Rest now, and know I will never, ever let anyone forget you and what you did for me."

I send the prayer up, hoping he hears it.

When I look back to the coffins, I see Cas watching me. I wipe the stray tears away and smile. He winks, knowing it's all the comfort he can give me right now, and it means a lot.

The coffins are all lowered into the ground. It's time to say goodbye.

I shudder from the slight chill sweeping across the cemetery. Once the dirt has been thrown on their coffins, Cas comes to my side and takes my hand. I've been holding onto five white roses, and I throw one on each of the three brothers I didn't know too well, saying a silent prayer for them as I do. Stopping in front of Micky's, I throw one down, and don't even try to wipe my tears.

"I love you, Uncle Micky. Rest in peace."

Rubbing my arm, Cas moves me along to Billy's grave.

My hand shakes as I throw down the last remaining rose. It's not enough, one flower and a weak apology.

"I'm sorry, my friend," I whisper.

My chest heaves as I try with all my might not to burst into ugly cries. Cas wraps me in his arms, shielding me from everyone's stares.

"Come on, let's get you out of here," he says, keeping his arm around my shoulders. By the time we get back to the cars, most of the crowd is back at their bikes.

As we drive away, they rev their engines and blast their horns in salute to their fallen brothers.

## Cas

I could see Alannah struggling to keep herself together throughout the service. I wish someone would have sat her away from Billy's grave; she couldn't keep her eyes off of it, apart from when she looked to the sky and her lips moved ever so slightly. I knew she was apologizing to him, again.

She needed me with her, but as President, I had my place at the front of my brothers, and that's where I had to stay.

I was breaking for her. As soon as the service was finished, I was at her side while she laid her roses, Micky's and Billy's hitting her the worst. I tried saving her from breaking down in front of everyone and got her back to the car as soon as I could.

Leading the way, I took my brothers home.

Back at the clubhouse, the music starts, and everyone has a drink in their hand. Inside and outside is both filled with brothers and women. The day turned to night, and under the dark, clouded sky, they continue to drink and share memories of the brothers we buried.

I've done enough roaming and making sure everyone's okay. I want my girl. I slip inside and scan the crowded bar for her, but she's not where I left her. She isn't anywhere in here. I check our room and find nothing, and she's not in the bathroom. I go back outside, still nowhere to be seen. My heart's doing fucking flips. Where the fuck is she?

My head swivels from side to side, looking everywhere.

"Check the roof."

I turn to see Sparky coming toward me.

"She always sneaks up there when it gets to be too much down here for her."

"Thanks, brother."

I round the clubhouse and find the ladder that leads to the roof. She shouldn't be up there. It isn't safe at all. Knowing Alannah, though, it would be more likely I would have to make it safe than to stop her from coming up here.

I'll never doubt my VP. She's sitting up here with her knees tucked into her chest.

I don't say anything until I'm next to her. Being up here must do her some good, as she looks a lot calmer now.

"You're not crying," I say happily.

"No. I can't do anything for them now. I've said goodbye, and anyway, if Micky was here to see me cry anymore for him, he would kick my ass," she laughs.

"I suppose he would," I agree. "It's okay to grieve for them, though. You don't have to hide anything from me. I know you're hurting."

"I know, but if I don't try and move on, I don't think I ever will. Like my father used to say: they knew the club, and they died for the club. It's the only way they would've wanted to go."

She's serious. Over the past week, I thought she might not get over this loss, but all she needed was closure of the funerals.

"Anyway, I have you now and everyone else. We have our future to look forward to." She smiles up at me.

I love hearing her say we have a future. I don't know what the future holds for us, but I know with everything I have that as long as it involves the club and Alannah, I'll be one happy fucker.

"Here, I have something for you." I pull out a box from inside my cut.

"You said you didn't want a crown, but you did ask for jewels."

I've never given a girl jewelry before, and never wanted to. I never thought they deserved it, but Alannah deserves every jewel on the planet.

She opens it and pulls out the necklace. Reading the inscription I had engraved on it first, she then turns it over and sees the diamond encrusted front.

"Cas's old lady forever," she giggles. "It's beautiful. Thank you," she coos, kissing me softly before passing it to me to put around her neck.

"One day soon, it'll be a ring in that box, and you'll never be able to leave me," I tell her.

"I'm not going anywhere," she promises.

Staring me in the eyes, she pushes against my chest until I'm lying on my back. Straddling me, she bends over and kisses me. I've missed her touch. I haven't made a move with her since she got hurt, patiently waiting until she was ready.

The way she grinds against my cock tells me she's more than ready now.

She reaches between us and undoes my jeans, so I lift my hips so she's able to pull my jeans down. I'm ready for her, and hard as a rock. My cock springs out from my boxers and pulses in her grip.

She doesn't even need me to get her going. Pulling her panties to the side, she positions herself above my cock and slides down on me slowly, soaking wet for me.

"I've missed you this way," she whispers against my neck as she moves herself in a slow, hypnotic rhythm.

"Me too, baby."

She clenches around me, and I nearly blow then and there. I want to flip her over and take control, but she's not completely healed, and against this roof, it could hurt her even more.

She continues to ride me and soaks every inch of my cock when she comes. I'm desperate for my own release, so I pull her tight to me and thrust into her with as much force as I can. Her pleasurable moans in my ear tip me over the edge, and I pour myself into her, not letting her go until I get my breathing back under control.

"That didn't last long," she giggles.

"Well, it's been forever since I was in there. Anyway, you came before I did," I tease her, knowing she's blushing.

"Like you said, it's been forever."

She moves off of me and grabs her purse, taking out her tissues and quickly wiping herself down before discarding the evidence.

"You ready to go back down?" I ask, buttoning my pants back up.

"I am now," she replies wistfully.

I try helping her down the ladder, but she slaps my hands away, though she does take my hand when we're both on the ground and walking back toward the crowd.

"It feels good, our relationship not being a secret anymore, doesn't it?"

"Sure does, babe."

Sure fucking does.

"When we wake up tomorrow, today will be a memory, and that's when life really begins to change," she murmurs closely.

She's right. We as brothers, and us as a club will change.

I pass Alannah over to Sparky and call for everyone's attention. Brothers begin coming out of the clubhouse and stand there, waiting for me to speak.

"Today, we say goodbye to our brothers, forever with us and never forgotten. To Ron, Shorty, Jonny 3, Micky, and Billy, we say goodbye, brothers. Rest in fucking peace." The crowd roars their farewells and raise their drinks to the sky.

"Tomorrow marks a new era for us, a new start, and we're going to fucking take it."

I take a bottle of beer being passed my way.

"Lost Souls till we die!" I yell and drink the bottle dry, thrusting the empty bottle into the air.

Taking my girl back under my arm, we drink the night away, welcoming the new era in together and into the next morning.

# EPILOGUE

A month has passed, and the club is healing slowly. I still haven't been able to go back to the cabin, and Cas assures me there's no rush. He's had to spend a lot of time at the club, and I know he feels better knowing I'm here.

I've surprised myself by making friends with a couple of the club girls. It's made me rethink my original opinion of them. Well, apart from the ones who do truly deserve my judgement.

Cas has been working hard repairing club business, relationships within it, and other connections. It turns out, Michael wasn't only betraying us, but other clubs and connections as well. But I don't ask. I don't need to know the details. All I need from Cas is him, and he's always willing to give me that. If we're in the same room and I want his attention, all I have to do is touch the necklace he gave me and bite my lip seductively. Even when he's extremely busy, he'll still give me his time.

With Cas as President, the clubhouse is busier than ever, with brothers staying even though they hadn't been called for business. Cas is bringing a new sense of brotherhood to the club, and the brothers like it.

So that's why tonight, I helped organise his becoming President party. Of course, we had our own private party while the girls finished setting up.

The bar area has been transformed with banners and decorations. I'd gone overboard, and had far too much alcohol delivered, but with new guests pouring in and out of the club on a daily basis, it won't go to waste.

It's the first celebration the club has seen in months. The music is blaring, the drinks never stop flowing, brothers are being serviced by the club girls whenever and wherever, and everyone is finally happy. Well, as happy as they can be, being stuck inside because of the rain.

"Hey, old man, how are you doing?" I ask Oak, sitting myself down on the stool next to him at the bar.

"I'm doing real good, darlin'." He smiles at me, then laughs when he catches me looking at Cas.

"That boy's gonna marry you real soon," he insists, seeing Cas smiling at me.

"I can't wait. I hope you'll be around to walk me up the aisle."

"I ain't going anywhere, darlin'. And I couldn't more honored that you'd ask me to take your daddy's place. He'd be proud of you coming through what you did, you know."

"I know. Guess we'll just have to wait for him to pop the question," I giggle, jumping down off the stool with a bottle of beer in each hand.

I kiss him quickly on the cheek and head back to Cas.

"I thought the President would like another beer," I giggle, handing him the bottle.

"Thanks, babe. Come here," he murmurs, tugging my hand to sit on his lap.

"No, no, no. You're going to dance with me."

I know he doesn't like to dance, but I know he'd hate it even more if I found someone else to dance with.

He rolls his eyes dramatically, but gets up and follows me to the dance area.

"I ain't doing none of the shit Sparky does with you," he warns.

I laugh at him. "I don't expect you to."

Putting my arms around his neck, he pulls me close and we simply sway to the music.

"I love you so much," I tell him.

"I love you more."

We continue to move in each other's arms, and when the song finishes, I expect him to say he's had enough, but he doesn't flinch. We carry on for what feels like forever.

Everything we've been through has only made us stronger. We lost each other for a year, and my abduction nearly separated us permanently. But we know what we have now, and neither of us are prepared to let it go.

"Cas."

It's not someone jokingly calling his name. We both hear the urgency in the voice and stop dancing.

A path clears between us and the door, and my eyes bulge when I see her standing there, bruised worse than I had been, and dripping head to toe from the rain with no jacket, only a bag hanging on her back.

I step closer to her. Once she sees me, she doesn't stop staring. She's out of breath, and her face is scrunched up in pain.

"Bonnie?" I murmur.

As soon as I say her name, everyone pulls their guns on her.

Who the fuck do they think she is?

"Y–you got a p–problem," she stammers as she shivers uncontrollably.

"Oh yeah? What problem would that be, darlin'?" Pope questions, moving closer with his gun trained on her.

"Your war isn't over. It's only just beginning."

Before anyone can say a word, she collapses to the floor.

## AVAILABLE NOW…

Biker Faith – Book 2 in the Lost Souls MC series available now.

Printed in Great Britain
by Amazon

26358013R00148